"Am I in trouble?"

He snapped his attention to her. "You're conscious."

"Disappointed, huh?" she teased.

Nate ripped his gaze from her adorable face. "This isn't funny."

"No, it most certainly is not. I was just doing my job and found a body. Is she dead? Please tell me she's not dead. At first I thought maybe she just collapsed and hit her head. I've passed out before from not remembering to eat."

Her nonstop chatter convinced Nate she was okay. "Cassie, take a breath."

"You're angry with me," she said.

"I'm not angry."

"You seem angry. Why, because I'm down here? I was only trying to get away." She hesitated. "That man, there was a man."

"It's okay, he's not here now. You're safe."

An eternal optimist, **Hope White** was born and raised in the Midwest. She and her college sweetheart have been married for thirty years and are blessed with two wonderful sons, two feisty cats and a bossy border collie. When not dreaming up inspirational tales, Hope enjoys hiking, sipping tea with friends and going to the movies. She loves to hear from readers, who can contact her at hopewhiteauthor@gmail.com.

Books by Hope White

Love Inspired Suspense

Echo Mountain

Mountain Rescue
Covert Christmas
Payback
Christmas Undercover
Witness Pursuit

Hidden in Shadows
Witness on the Run
Christmas Haven
Small Town Protector
Safe Harbor

Visit the Author Profile page at Harlequin.com.

WITNESS PURSUIT

HOPE WHITE

HARLEQUIN® LOVE INSPIRED® SUSPENSE

Recycling programs
for this product may
not exist in your area.

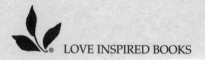

LOVE INSPIRED BOOKS

ISBN-13: 978-0-373-44767-1

Witness Pursuit

www.Harlequin.com

Printed in U.S.A.

Wherefore putting away lying, speak every man truth with his neighbor: for we are members one of another.
–Ephesians 4:25

For Lar, my real-life hero

ONE

Cassie McBride got out of Ruby, her little red car, and froze.

The front door to the Whispering Pines cabin was ajar. That wasn't right. Was the renter still on the premises? How awkward. The woman was supposed to have checked out by noon and it was nearly eight o'clock in the evening.

Cassie pulled out her phone to call Becca, her best friend. Becca had helped Cassie get the job as a property manager for Echo Mountain Rentals, which rented out private cabins to vacationers in the Cascade Mountains. Perhaps Becca had dealt with this type of situation and could offer advice.

No, if Cassie wanted people to think of her as independent, she needed to act more and ask less. She decided not to bring in the fresh linens and toiletries until she'd resolved this issue. Who knows, she might even have to call security.

"Be strong," she coached, but she abhorred conflict. If she were to keep this good-paying job, she'd have to do the uncomfortable tasks like kick out renters who'd overstayed their welcome. She straightened her shoulders, marched to the front door and eased it open. "Hello? It's the property manager."

Silence.

"Anyone here?"

Nothing.

She sighed with relief. Perhaps the door didn't latch properly when the renter vacated the premises.

Her gaze drifted to the picture window and the incredible view of the Cascade Mountains. She would miss these mountains when she left on her travel adventures overseas where she'd discover new mountains and beautiful places in foreign lands.

But she wasn't there yet.

To get the cabin ready for tomorrow's renters, she pulled her phone out of her purple bag and opened the checklist. She glanced toward the back of the house and noticed the patio door wasn't locked.

"Not a very responsible renter," she said to herself. She'd let Mr. Anderson know not to rent to that woman again. She crossed the room and locked the door.

Turning her attention to the kitchen, Cassie got busy with her assignment. Her report needed to be filed tonight, and if anything was damaged they'd send maintenance to fix the problem before the next renter checked in.

To help her focus, she plugged earbuds into her phone and hit Play. This was the perfect job for Cassie, and she couldn't thank Becca enough for recommending her to her boss. The money earned during the high season would pad Cassie's bank account so she could escape Echo Mountain sooner rather than later.

Starting in the kitchen, Cassie turned the appliances on and off—the toaster, blender and microwave. She checked the garbage disposal and oven. All seemed in working order.

During a break between songs, she thought she heard something. It sounded like scratching. Another song started, and Cassie hit Pause. Pulled out the earbuds.

Scratch, scratch, whine.

She followed the source of the sound into the master bedroom.

Whine, whine, scratch.

It was coming from the closet. Thinking a critter might have sneaked in through the open door, she grabbed a pillow off the bed, ready to shoo it out of the house.

She took a deep breath, counted to three and slid the door open.

A flash of fur dashed out of the closet.

Cassie gasp-shrieked, startled by the sudden movement of a little dog sprinting across the room. She caught her breath, her gaze trained on the terrier mix scurrying into the master bathroom.

"Where did you come from, Dasher?" The name seemed appropriate, although not so much his presence. Whispering Pines was a no-pet property. Cassie followed him, stepped into the bathroom doorway and froze.

A limp female body lay sprawled across the edge of the Jacuzzi tub.

"Oh no, ma'am?"

Cassie rushed to the fully clothed unconscious woman. As she knelt beside her, Cassie noticed blood trailing down the side of the woman's face. Had she hit her head? Cassie felt for a pulse, but couldn't find one. The dog barked frantically as if trying to revive its master.

"Gotta get help." Cassie ran into the kitchen, the dog practically underfoot. She could barely think over the constant barking, so she picked up the dog to soothe him. "It's okay, buddy," she said, stroking his head.

She grabbed her smartphone off the counter, and with trembling fingers she called 911.

"911 Emergency," the operator answered.

"My name is Cassie McBride. There's a woman, she's injured, maybe dead I'm not sure, in Whispering Pines cabin on Reflection Pass Drive."

"What's the address, ma'am?"

"I... I... Hang on a second." Cassie fiddled with the phone, opening a map program. Becca had given her landmarks, not an actual address, when she'd asked Cassie to cover for her tonight.

The map program was taking too long to load. A woman could be dying in the next room.

She held the phone to her ear once again. "Just take the first right after Craig's Gas and Grub on Highway Two, then a left at the blue bear mailbox and you'll see the cabin up ahead."

"Ma'am, we need an address."

"I don't have it. I'll have to call my manager and call you back."

"Ma'am, I need you to stay on the line. Give me your manager's phone number."

Cassie rattled it off.

"We'll get in touch with him," the dispatcher said. "Please tell me what happened."

"I'm a property manager and was checking one of our rentals and I heard scratching. It was a dog and he ran out of the closet and into the bathroom and when I followed him, I... I found an unconscious woman. You need to send someone, quick!"

Cassie hoped she was making sense, but adrenaline flooded her brain and jumbled her thoughts. She took a few steps into the main living area, hoping the peaceful view would ground her somehow. She glanced out the window...

And spotted a man heading toward the cabin carrying a shovel over his shoulder.

She dropped to the floor, clutching the little dog.

"Someone's here," she whispered into the phone.

"Who's there?"

"A man, he's coming toward the house with a shovel. What is he doing with a shovel? Oh my God, he dug a grave, he dug a grave and he's going to bury her."

"Ma'am, please stay calm."

"I need to get out of here. I'll leave the line open, but I can't talk. And don't talk to me because he might hear you." She pocketed the phone and crouch-walked across the living room, carrying the dog under her arm like a pro quarterback clutching a football.

She swallowed her panic, her fear. Maybe he wasn't a killer preparing to dispose of a body. Maybe he was with maintenance doing a little grounds work. No, he wasn't in a dark green uniform. He wore jeans, a black T-shirt and a leather jacket.

Cassie needed out of here. She needed to get safe. Glancing at the kitchen counter, she eyed her keys lying beside her bag. Just as she started toward them she heard the rattling at the back door. He was there, trying to get in. She'd locked him out, which meant he knew someone was inside.

She was inside.

And if she reached for her keys now, he'd see her for sure.

Dread gripped her chest. She was next.

She counted to three. Calmed her breathing.

She hadn't survived a childhood fraught with illness to become a victim of random violence. She had things to do and places to explore, places on the other side of the world that she'd promised herself she'd visit once her health stabilized.

She stroked the dog's soft fur, which both helped keep him quiet and calmed her fear.

The door rattled. More violently this time.

Maybe the police would get here before he broke in. Maybe—

A crash was followed by a click and footsteps.

Cowering in the entryway, she heard floorboards squeak as he crossed the room. The sound of keys scraping against the kitchen counter sent a shudder of fear down her spine.

He'd found her keys. He knew she was still here.

She had seconds until…

The pounding of footsteps sprinted toward the bedroom. Of course, where he thought he'd find Cassie, the intruder, potential witness to murder.

This was her chance.

She slid open the side window and climbed through, still clinging to the dog. Only then did she realize taking care of Dasher was keeping her somewhat sane.

Once outside, she sprinted in the opposite direction of the master bedroom, assuming the guy might come looking for her.

If only she could escape in her car, but that was impossible without her keys. She focused on her breathing, taking slow, calming breaths.

The dog released a quick bark. "No, Dasher, no bark."

She spotted a trail up ahead leading to the next property, about half a mile away.

Half a mile. She could do it. She wouldn't be the victim of circumstance, a victim of "wrong place, wrong time." There were so many things she had yet to accomplish, things she ached to experience.

Like love.

As she ran steadily, the dog flopping in her arms, she scolded herself for losing focus and thinking about such trivialities. Yet with danger barreling down on her, she was haunted by her biggest fear: she would never experience romantic love.

Because her childhood illness had left her so damaged that no one would want her.

Knock it off, she mentally scolded herself. This kind of thinking would not keep her alive.

She made it to the trail and clenched her jaw with determination, thinking what a great story she'd be able to tell her friends when this was over. When she was safe.

Towering trees reached for the sky on either side of her; the trail was well worn and easy to navigate. Which meant if she could navigate it, so could Shovel Man. She glanced over her shoulder. Didn't see anything.

She turned back to the trail. Increased her speed.

A few minutes later he called out to her. "Hey! Stop!"

He knew she was there, running for her life. She skidded as she took a sharp turn, but caught herself and managed not to slide over the edge into the abyss below.

She peeked to her right, down into the steep drop, and it gave her an idea. If she could find a way down at the next turn, her pursuer might think she'd continued on the trail. Yes, that's it.

Somehow she needed to disappear, and quickly. She uncoiled her scarf from around her neck and wrapped the dog in it, then secured him against her chest. Thank God he was a little guy, probably seven pounds soaking wet. This was not something she could do with a golden retriever like Fiona, her sister's dog.

"Let's go, Dasher." Cassie peered over the edge. She needed to stay out of sight only until police arrived. "Emergency, this is Cassie McBride," she said, speaking into the phone, still in her shirt pocket. "I'm climbing down the mountain to a safe spot, out of view."

"Is the perpetrator following you?"

"Yes, I think so. I'm about a quarter of a mile south of the cabin. Send help." She eyed the perfect spot to grab a tree root and lower herself.

"Deep breathing, doggie," she coached, as if the dog understood her. She grabbed the tree root jutting out from the mountainside, and lowered herself until she found a firm rock on which to plant her feet. The next step would be landing on a small ledge, about ten feet below.

"Just like REI," she said, referring to a rock-climbing class she'd taken months ago.

She took a slow, deep breath. She could do this.

With a grunt, she edged her right foot onto a thick tree branch sticking out from the mountain wall. She reached for another branch to hold on to.

The branch beneath her foot snapped.

And she dropped.

Police Chief Nate Walsh had a firm grip of one end of the stretcher, and Eddie Monroe had the other. As a search-and-rescue volunteer, a sense of satisfaction gave Nate the added strength necessary to make the final trek down the mountain carrying the injured woman.

It was a good thing they got to her when they did, since it would be dark soon. Darkness would have made the mission more challenging, even though her injuries weren't life-threatening.

Although some folks in town had expected him to give up his SAR work when he was named police chief last year, helping people, saving them from the dangers of the wild, gave Nate a sense of control over the random chaos of life.

Random, like his partner's death nearly four years ago on the Chicago PD. Perhaps if Nate had known where Dean's head was at he'd still be alive, along with the witness Dean had been protecting.

The witness Dean had fallen in love with.

If Nate had only known, he would have convinced his partner to not let something like love cloud his judgment and ruin his career. Which was probably why his partner decided not to share.

Sometimes people considered Nate's firm opinions as judgmental, yet he was about protecting family and friends. Besides, Nate wouldn't be arrogant enough to pass judgment, since he was far from perfect.

These days he'd strive to be as close to perfect as possible for the citizens of Echo Mountain. Volunteering for SAR kept him connected with his community, even if some of these folks wondered how he had the time given his chief duties.

He and Eddie carried the wounded hiker, a twentysomething female named Sylvia, to the command center where an emergency vehicle waited.

"Thanks, thanks, everyone," Sylvia said. "Thanks, Chief."

"You're welcome. Take care of yourself."

"Chief," SAR volunteer Luke Winters said. "Dispatch needs you to call in."

"Thanks." He shook hands with a few of the volunteers and went to his truck. When he'd taken over as chief, he'd directed dispatch to give him immediate updates on criminal activity calls, however minor. Kids in a small town had a tendency to grow bored and get into mischief.

He fired up his truck and pulled away from the command center, grateful for the successful mission. Another life saved.

"Dispatch, this is Chief Walsh, over."

"Sir, there's been a 911 call reporting a wounded, possibly dead body, and the female witness says the killer is still on the premises, over."

Adrenaline rushed through his bloodstream. "Address?"

"We're looking it up, over."

"The witness couldn't tell you?" What kind of fruitcake didn't know where she was?

"She had directions, but no address. She works for Echo Mountain Rentals, over."

Nate's blood ran cold. Cassie worked for Echo Mountain Rentals. Cassie, his best friend's sister with the sparkling blue eyes and a contagious smile.

"Did the caller give you her name?"

"Cassie McBride."

Nate gripped the radio so hard he thought it might crack in his hand.

"I need that address, over," he said.

"One minute, over."

He didn't have a minute. A sweet, lighthearted young woman who looked at the world through a veil of optimism was in trouble. Cassie trusted too easily and believed in the goodness of all and the glory of God.

She hadn't been tainted by life's tragedies, and wouldn't be able to cope with a crisis, much less a violent perp.

"The address?" Nate snapped, pulling onto Highway Two.

"5427 Reflection Pass Drive. We still have an open line to her phone, over."

"Patch it through, over," he said.

"Yes, sir, over."

"Alert all available officers. Did you dispatch an ambulance, over?"

"Yes, sir, over."

Nate gripped the steering wheel with his left hand and held on to the radio with his right. Coordinates indicated he was about five minutes out.

Hang on, Cassie. I'm coming.

What was she doing up there at this time of night? She should be relaxing in her apartment above the tea shop with a good book, not working. Then he remembered why she'd taken a second, part-time job with the rental company: to earn money for travel.

The thought of her traveling alone didn't sit well with Nate or her big brother, Aiden. If she could stumble into trouble in her own hometown, Nate shuddered to think what could happen to her in a foreign country.

But she wasn't gone, not yet. She was in danger right here in Echo Mountain. Nate pressed down on the accelerator and flipped the lights. It might get folks talking, but he didn't care.

All he cared about was getting to Cassie. Making sure she was okay.

His phone rang, and he recognized Aiden's number.

"Chief Walsh," he answered.

"Sorry to bother you, but my little sister was supposed to stop by Mom's and she's late and hasn't called."

"I'm heading up to Reflection Pass now."

"Reflection Pass? Why?"

"Cassie called 911," Nate said.

"What's wrong? Is she okay?"

"I'll let you know as soon as I get to her. Just hang tight."

"Where is she? I'm coming."

Just then, sounds from Cassie's phone echoed over the radio.

"I've gotta go." Nate ended the call. He held his breath as he listened.

"Deep breathing, doggie," Cassie's gentle voice whispered through the radio.

Nate's fingers wrapped tighter around the steering wheel. "Just like REI," she said.

He realized she was climbing down the mountain to get away from danger.

"Cassie, no," he ground out. She didn't have proper gear and wasn't a seasoned climber.

A few seconds later, a soft shriek echoed through his car. His heart pounded against his chest. What happened? Did she fall?

"Where did you go?" a male voice called.

The perp was there? Stalking her? Nate slammed his palm against the steering wheel.

"Cassie McBride?" the man called.

How did he know her name? Nate grabbed the radio. "Dispatch, how close are the patrol cars to Reflection Pass Drive, over?"

"About a minute out, over."

"Tell them to hit the sirens."

"Copy that."

A woman's moan floated across the inside of his truck. He glanced at the radio, then back at the road. Two minutes; he had to be only two minutes out.

"Is that you down there?" a man said.

Nate flipped on his siren and floored it.

The next few minutes were a blur. It took all of Nate's self-control to keep the panic from turning him into a raving lunatic. He reined in his temper. Locals had been worried about giving the chief's position to a thirtysomething like Nate, from a big city. Folks didn't think he had the patience for being chief of a small town.

He was determined to prove them wrong. Echo Mountain had become his home. He'd moved here three years ago to support his sister and her teenage son. He'd been absent from their lives far too long, playing protector for the rest of the world. He'd been pretty good at it, until he'd failed Dean.

He would not fail Cassie.

As he pulled onto Reflection Pass Drive, two patrol cars turned the corner up ahead. Nate sped toward the house, parking behind Cassie's little red car. He whipped his door open and motioned to officers James "Red" Carrington and Ryan McBride. "Red, search the house. McBride, you're with me."

Nate hoped that seeing her cousin Ryan McBride might comfort Cassie. Red drew his weapon and entered the house.

Nate grabbed rope from his trunk, then called dispatch. "I need the last known location for Cassie McBride, over."

"Quarter of a mile south of the cabin, over."

The ambulance peeled up the driveway and the paramedics hopped out; one was Cassie's cousin, and Ryan's sister, Maddie McBride.

"Wait until Officer Carrington gives the all clear." Nate took off toward the trail, Officer McBride right behind him.

Nate withdrew his firearm. The guy still had to be here, right? Jogging up the trail, Nate steadied his breath, occasionally glancing over the edge. She could be anywhere down there.

The trail forked, and Nate pointed for Officer McBride to go left. Nate continued another few minutes.

The sound of a barking dog echoed from below. Nate knelt to look over the edge.

"Cassie! Cassie, you down there?"

The barking intensified, but there was no response from Cassie.

Had the guy climbed down there and…

Nate would not allow himself to go there. He holstered his gun and secured the rope around a tree trunk nearby. He had to get down there and make sure she was okay.

Because if she wasn't…

Something slammed against Nate's back and he lurched forward, over the edge.

TWO

Nate had experienced his share of falls, and that experience taught him how to survive even in impossible situations. As he tumbled off the trail gripping the rope he'd secured to the trunk, his back smacked against the mountain wall. He clenched his jaw against the pain. He glanced up, but didn't see his attacker peering over the edge.

"McBride!" he called out to his junior officer, as Nate clung precariously to the rope.

Silenced echoed back at him. He planted his boots against the mountain wall and lowered himself. A few seconds later, a splash of bright blue caught his eye below, in contrast to the rich green surroundings.

Cassie. It had to be. She usually wore bright colors, much like her bright personality.

Totally inappropriate time to be thinking about her fashion choices, Nate.

"Cassie?" he said, getting closer.

Nothing. He released the rope and dropped to the ledge. He was desperate to check on Cassie, but needed to alert his men.

"This is Chief Walsh," he said into the radio. "The perpetrator is still on the premises, over."

"Are you okay, over?" Red said.

"Affirmative. McBride, check in, over."

Silence.

"Red, we need backup. Call County, over."

"Ten-four."

Although Ryan McBride was an exceptional police officer, Nate worried that the perp had surprised and attacked Ryan before coming after Nate.

The dog growled, protective of the woman he guarded.

Nate knelt beside Cassie. "Good dog. Now let me have a look."

She lay on her side, unconscious. "Cassie?"

He hesitated before checking her pulse. *Don't be stupid. She's a young, healthy woman. A fall like this wouldn't kill her.*

Pressing his fingers against her neck, he caught himself wanting to ask God for a favor, not for Nate, of course, because he knew better, but for Cassie.

Her pulse tapped steadily against his fingertips. He took a deep breath. With a trembling finger, he trailed golden-blond strands of hair off her cheek. Redness discolored her head above her right eye, but he didn't see any lacerations. He wished she'd open her eyes.

"Chief, what's your twenty, over?" Red asked.

"About a quarter mile south of the cabin off the trail on the right. We'll need SAR to lift Cassie McBride off a ledge, over."

"Aiden McBride is already here, over."

"Of course he is," Nate muttered to himself. "What about Officer McBride?" he said into the radio.

"He hasn't checked in, over."

"Be on the lookout, over."

"Ten-four."

Nate glanced across the mountain range. The sun had already started its descent. He wanted to get Cassie off this ledge so they wouldn't have to do this in the dark.

"Am I in trouble?"

He snapped his attention to her. "You're conscious."

"Disappointed, huh?" she teased.

Nate ripped his gaze from her adorable face. "This isn't funny."

"No, it most certainly is not. I was just doing my job and found a body. Is she dead? Please tell me she's not dead. At first I thought maybe she just collapsed and hit her head. I've passed out before from not remembering to eat."

Her nonstop chatter convinced Nate she was okay. "Cassie, take a breath."

Cassie and Nate couldn't be more different. While many thought of Nate as a reserved enigma, Cassie was bubbly and upbeat. Her brother, Nate's friend Aiden, said she'd drive any man crazy with her constant questions and observations about life, especially a man like Nate.

Drive him crazy? Sometimes, yet other times he enjoyed the pleasant sound of her voice.

"You're angry with me," she said.

"I'm not angry."

"You seem angry. Why, because I'm down here? I was only trying to get away." She hesitated. "That man, there was a man."

"It's okay, he's not here now. You're safe."

"He was carrying a shovel and broke into the house and—"

"Cassie." He placed a hand on her shoulder. "You're okay. I'm here and your brother's on his way with rescue gear."

She sighed. "Great, Aiden and his lectures. Look, I'm fine." She sat up and winced, gripping her head. "This must be what a hangover feels like."

Of course, she wouldn't know firsthand because she never drank, unlike Nate, who at one point found himself using alcohol to ease the sting of grief and the bitter taste of shame.

That was another reason he didn't like spending too much time around Cassie—he worried he'd somehow sully her goodness.

"I'm glad you're here," she said.

He snapped his attention to her, trying to read her expression. Was she teasing? Because he knew he often came off like a jerk, abrupt and cold.

She watched him, as if waiting for him to respond to her comment.

He had no response, fearing if he opened his mouth he'd give her a lecture about being out so late alone.

"Are you okay?" she said.

Something snapped.

"Am *I* okay?"

The dog jumped into her lap, and she stroked its fur. "Yeah, you look more worried than usual, and your shirt's torn and you're clenching your fist like you want to hit a punching bag at Bracken's Gym. So it's logical to ask if you're okay, not that you consider my questions logical but—"

"No, Cassie, I'm not okay," he interrupted. "What were you thinking coming out here so late?"

"It's only eight o'clock."

"But by yourself without protection?"

"What, like a bodyguard?" She smiled.

Which only frustrated him more.

"It's Echo Mountain," she said. "Besides, I have pepper spray in my bag, not that I could get to it because it was on the counter and I was hiding in the front hallway."

"Pepper spray?" he said.

"Yeah."

"You think pepper spray is going to protect you from guys like this?"

"Guys like what? I don't even know who he was."

"Well, he knows you." He immediately regretted his words when her face went white.

"How is that possible?" she said.

"Didn't you hear him calling your name from above?"

She shook her head. "How did you hear him?"

"You left your phone on. Dispatch put it through. Speaking of which, give me your phone." He stuck out his hand.

The dog dived between Nate and Cassie, frantically barking.

"It's okay, Dasher," Cassie said. "He's not really angry.

That's just Chief Walsh." She restrained the dog with one hand and gave Nate her phone with the other.

"Dispatch, this is Chief Walsh. I'm with Cassie McBride. Rescue is on the way. I'm closing the line, over." He handed it back to her.

"If you give me a boost I can climb back up and save search-and-rescue from having to come get me."

"I'd rather you relax until they arrive."

"This is silly." She struggled to stand.

Since she wasn't going to listen to him, Nate reached out to steady her. That's when he noticed the blood smearing her sleeve.

"Cassie, did you touch the body in the cabin?"

"Only to feel for a pulse, why?"

"You've got blood on your jacket." He motioned to her sleeve.

"Oh, wow, I didn't see that before. You'd think I would have noticed, especially since it's so...bright." Her legs buckled.

Nate caught her as she went down, the dog wedged between them. He lowered her to the ground and examined the wound. It wasn't bad, yet it had caused her to pass out. Concerned, he ran his hands over her clothes searching for other wounds, but found none.

Then he remembered her reaction when her brother had suffered a knife wound last year.

"Can't handle the sight of blood," he said under his breath.

It was okay; she was okay. He examined her wound closer. The four-inch gash didn't look deep. She probably snagged her arm on a sharp branch on her descent.

He pulled gauze from the earlier rescue out of his jacket and wrapped her wound as the dog hovered close by. They hadn't even discussed how she'd ended up with the dog. He knew she didn't own a dog, because it would interfere with her travel plans. Which meant she'd rescued a dog while being stalked by a killer and rappelled down the side of a mountain with the pup in her arms. This woman was…

"Nate, the team's here," Aiden called from above.

"Great!" Nate called back.

Cassie awoke in an ambulance, confused and worried.

"Where's Dasher?" she asked her cousin Madeline, the EMT.

"Who?"

"My dog."

"You don't have a dog."

"I had him on the ledge with me. What happened to him? You didn't just let him go, did you? He could get eaten by wild animals or—"

"I didn't do anything but tend to the laceration on your arm and check your vitals. You were passed out cold. Didn't even wake up when they strapped you to a litter and lifted you up the mountain."

"I need to find Dasher."

"Cassie—"

"Please Madeline, I need to find him!"

"Calm down. I'll have Rocky call and check on the dog, okay?"

Cassie nodded, unsure why she was freaking out about a little dog that wasn't even hers. But there was something about him—his protectiveness and vulnerability—that made her feel connected to the terrier mix.

Then there was the way Chief Walsh interacted with Dasher, how Nate's tone softened when he praised the dog for protecting Cassie.

Good dog. Now let me have a look.

She'd heard him speak, although she thought she was dreaming at the time. Then she cracked open her eyes and saw Chief Walsh's intense expression studying her. With a gentle touch, he brushed hair off her face. Who would have guessed such a hardened man could be so caring?

She blinked away a tear. She was being ridiculous, yet the truth was she'd felt safe when he touched her. All the trepidation that flooded her system had dissolved in the very instant she felt the warmth of his fingertips against her cheek.

"What's wrong?" Madeline asked.

"What do you mean?"

"You're crying."

"Allergies."

"Cassie," Madeline said in that motherly tone, the tone everyone in Cassie's family used when speaking to her.

That's why she needed to get out of town, to explore other places in the world where people didn't know her as Baby McBride with the strange autoimmune disease.

"Cassie?" Madeline pressed.

"I'm fine," she said, closing her eyes.

"You're not fine. Do you want to talk about it?"

"Nothing to talk about."

"Finding a dead body—"

Cassie's eyes popped open. "So she *was* dead?"

"You didn't know?"

Cassie shook her head.

"I'm sorry." Madeline patted Cassie's shoulder.

It was just the beginning, Cassie thought, the beginning of her family and friends smothering her until she could no longer breathe.

God, please help me cope.

She suspected all the prayer in the world wouldn't change the way people looked at her: like a fragile doll, a sick little girl who could barely manage on her own. But she wasn't a little girl anymore, and she'd outgrown her illness, although the technical term was *remission*.

That fact wouldn't change the way people treated her. She decided to take the offensive.

"Have you assessed my injuries?" she asked her cousin.

"Your arm will need a few stiches, and the ER doc will probably order a CT scan of your head."

"I didn't hit my head."

"You might not remember hitting your head, but you're exhibiting symptoms of head trauma."

"Like what?"

"Obsessing over a random dog."

"An orphaned dog."

"And you're anxious."

"Rocky's driving too fast."

Madeline shook her head and bit back a smile. "Rocky, this is base, over," a voice said over the radio.

"Go ahead."

"Chief Walsh has the dog, over."

"You hear that, Cassie?" Rocky said over his shoulder.

"Yeah, thanks."

"Okay?" Madeline said.

Cassie nodded and closed her eyes, wanting to avoid arguing with her cousin. She'd save her energy because she knew there'd be more discussion, more arguments about her choices today as she defended herself to her mother, older brother, sister and whoever else jumped on the "help Cassie" bandwagon.

She thought about her bank account, now up to two thousand dollars and change. It wasn't enough to support herself for six months to a year overseas, even if she stayed in hostels. After tonight's fiasco, she might lose the awesome-paying property manager job. At the very least, her family would forbid her from going anywhere by herself for a while.

They reached the hospital, and Rocky and Madeline wheeled Cassie inside. Once transferred to an ER bed, Madeline slid the curtain closed.

"The doctor will be here shortly. I think Dr. Rush is on duty. You'll like her," Madeline said.

"I need to speak with Chief Walsh."

"Oh yeah?" Maddie said with a raised eyebrow.

"Stop fooling around. It's important."

"I think he's at the cabin managing the investigation into the woman's death."

"Oh, right." Cassie wanted to call and give him a description of Shovel Man. She reached into her pocket. "Where's my phone? Can you check the ambulance?"

"Sure, if you promise to stay here and wait for the doctor."

"As opposed to going dancing?"

"See? Sarcastic. That's not like you, which is why I suspect a head injury. So relax. I'll be right back."

Cassie laid her head against the pillow and closed her eyes. She knew she didn't have a serious head injury, and was upset that her cousin wasn't listening to her. Cassie needed to call Chief Walsh and describe the man who'd stalked her. She could still picture those heavy eyebrows and thin lips. He reminded her of Mr. Gruner, a curmudgeon who used to yell at Cassie and her friends whenever they'd pass by his boat at the Emerald Lake Pier. They were terrified of him, until the day he saved Izzy Bingham. No one knew Izzy couldn't swim. After the save, the kids had changed their opinions of Mr. Gruner. He was just lonely, not mean.

She had a feeling Shovel Man didn't fall into that same category.

A shiver snaked down her arms. She slipped into her jacket to get warm. The more agitated she appeared, the more her family would close ranks and suffocate her. She had to show them she was strong, healthy and capable, that she wasn't that sick little girl anymore.

The curtain slid open.

"Did you find it?" she said, assuming it was Madeline.

"I'm here to take you for a CT scan," a male voice said.

"Oh, okay."

She opened her eyes, but he stood behind her as he pushed her bed out of the examining area.

"I was hoping you were my cousin with my phone," she said.

"Nope, sorry."

"How long does a CT scan take?"

"Not long."

She knew they wouldn't find anything, but she couldn't fault the doctor for being cautious. They entered the elevator, and he pressed the button for the bottom floor.

"How did you get injured?" he said.

She glanced at the orderly, who wore a surgical mask. A surgical mask?

"I've got a cold," he said in explanation.

Yet even behind the mask she recognized the thick eyebrows of the man who'd been carrying the shovel.

The elevator doors closed.

THREE

Cassie was alone with the killer.

A ball of fear rose in her chest.

No, she wasn't going to give up without a fight.

She had nothing with which to defend herself, nor did she have her phone to call for help. But she was a smart woman and would use her best weapons: her wits and her words.

She took a quick breath for strength. Wait, she remembered she had her emergency house keys in her side pocket. Locking herself out last month had become a blessing after all. She launched into chatter mode to distract him.

"I can't believe they want a CT scan," she started. "I told them I didn't hit my head. I can see just fine and I know my own name."

"So what happened?"

"I'm a klutz. I fell off a trail. Can you believe that?" She deftly reached into her jacket to palm the keys. "I mean, I've lived here forever and Dad used to take us hiking, and you'd think I'd be an expert with all my experience, but I wasn't paying attention and went over the side of the mountain. Isn't that the most ridiculous thing you've ever heard?"

"Why weren't you paying attention?" he asked.

She slipped the keys between her fingers, thinking she could jab him in the eye if necessary. "I was scared," she said.

"Of what?"

"I'd found an unconscious woman at a rental house and there was all this blood." She shuddered.

"Was she dead?"

"I have no idea, but me and blood? Not a good mix. Last year my brother was attacked by a guy with a knife and there was blood everywhere, all over the kitchen, and I completely freaked out. I guess that's what happened today.

I took off and lost my footing and fell off the trail. Quite embarrassing if you think about it."

She hoped she could convince him she hadn't seen his face at the cabin. She certainly didn't want to get into hand-to-key combat.

She clutched the keys tighter. "Have you ever done anything dumb? It would make me feel a whole lot better if you had."

"Nothing comes to mind."

The doors opened and he wheeled her out of the elevator. Jumping off and running didn't seem like the best plan, since he was much taller than Cassie and therefore a lot faster. She strategized her next move as she chatted away.

"I'm going to get a huge lecture from my family, but what else is new?" she said, laying it on thick. "I'm the flaky one. This won't surprise them one bit. The woman probably fell and hit her head, yet I freaked and tore off like a scared cat. Oh well, at least I wasn't totally irresponsible, because I called 911 for help."

She pretended to be relaxed, not easy considering Shovel Man's hands were pushing her from behind—hands of a killer hovering dangerously close to her throat.

Dear Lord, give me wisdom and courage to know how to convince this man he does not have to take another life. My life.

That's when she spotted a fire alarm on the wall. Perfect.

She suddenly sat up and sniffed. "Wait, do you smell that?"

"What?"

"I smell smoke!" She hopped off the bed and yanked the alarm.

She took off running and glanced over her shoulder. Shovel Man stood there with a quizzical frown.

"Hurry!" she shouted. She had to keep up the pretense that she thought he was an orderly, not a killer.

Staff rushed out of rooms and flooded the hallway, puzzling over the alarm. Shovel Man was no doubt puzzled, as well. But at least she was away from him.

She shot another quick glance behind her.

He'd disappeared.

Relief settled in her chest, but only for a second. If he could disappear that quickly, he could reappear just as fast. Or worse, what if he was working with a partner who was waiting outside in a car to whisk Cassie away? Shovel Man could have given his partner Cassie's description: short with blond hair, wearing a bright blue jacket.

As she marched toward the exit, she shucked her jacket, wincing in pain from her injured arm.

Once outside, she tossed the jacket onto a bench and practically sprinted into the parking lot.

But where should she go? She didn't know which of these strangers she could trust, and didn't have her phone to call for help.

Across the parking lot she spotted the one place she knew she'd be safe, Nate's truck. Which meant he had to be close. Scanning the parking lot, she didn't see Nate, only frantic employees and patients being herded out of the north side of the building.

Feeling badly about causing the commotion, she waved down an orderly who was arriving for work. "It's a false alarm. I pulled it because someone's after me. Tell them they don't have to evacuate the building!"

She ran off, hoping he'd relay the message before too many patients were inconvenienced. Head down, she motored toward Nate's truck and tried the door, but it was locked. She climbed into the flatbed. It seemed like the best place to hide.

Truth was, she felt safe because it was Nate's truck. Eventually he'd have to return to it, and he'd find her.

The reality of what just happened shot a chill down her spine: Cassie had faced off with a suspected killer. Her hands started trembling, then her arms and legs. She gasped for breath, determined to stay conscious.

Nate shoved down the panic threatening to pull him off course.

Cassie was missing.

He clenched his jaw and retraced her steps through the hospital, hoping to find a clue as to where she'd gone.

Hoping to find her safe and sound in a hospital room.

Instead, it was like she'd vanished in the mist.

The hospital alarm suddenly clicked off. Through the ominous silence, his fear grew louder, more insistent: *She's been taken against her will. She's been killed and her body will be found in a laundry bin.*

He had to stop these torturous thoughts and think like a detective–turned–chief of police.

"Why'd the alarm go off?" he asked into his radio.

"I'm checking, sir."

Nate had locked down the cabin crime scene, called the lab tech and brought Officer Ryan McBride to the hospital to get checked out. He'd been assaulted and suffered a head wound. Nate assumed from the guy who shoved him off the trail.

Anyone could have driven McBride into town, but Nate wanted to check on Cassie.

"Apparently it was a false alarm, over," Red called through the radio.

"How do you know that?" Nate asked.

"A staff member encountered the woman who pulled the alarm."

"Why would she—" Instinct struck him square in the chest. "What did this woman look like?"

"Blond, short, twenties."

"Where did he see her?"

"Back entrance, heading into the parking lot."

Nate rushed to the exit, wondering if Cassie had pulled the alarm because she'd been in trouble.

"Should we continue checking the lower level?" Red asked.

"No, meet me in the back parking lot. And bring the employee who spoke with her."

"Copy that."

Nate jogged outside, navigating the sea of staff members headed back into the hospital. What made Cassie pull the alarm?

He scanned the parking lot for her wavy blond hair. Had she changed into a hospital gown, or was she still wearing her electric blue jacket? That would make her easy to spot.

Out of the corner of his eye, a pop of blue caught his attention. He went to a nearby bench and picked up Cassie's jacket.

"Chief?"

Nate glanced to his left. Red and an orderly approached.

"This is Kevin Wright, the man who spoke with the woman who pulled the alarm," Red introduced.

Nate pulled out his phone and found a picture of Cassie and Aiden taken at the Christmas Lights Festival last year. He flashed the image at the orderly. "Is this the woman you spoke with?"

"Yes sir."

"When did you see her?" Nate asked.

"About ten minutes ago."

"What did she say to you, exactly?"

"That she pulled the alarm because someone was after her."

Nate's fingers dug into the down-filled jacket. "Who was after her?"

"She didn't say."

"Where was she going?"

"She took off into the parking lot." He pointed. "That way."

"Thank you." Nate dismissed the orderly and pulled Red

aside. "Put out a BOLO on Cassie McBride. See how fast a few of the guys can get here to help search the woods bordering the parking lot."

"You think he dumped her body—"

"Call Spike and Harvey," Nate cut him off.

"What about SAR?"

"Too many personal connections."

"You mean Aiden and Bree?"

"Let's leave them out of this for now."

"I think it's too late for that." Red nodded at Aiden, who sprinted toward them.

"What happened?" Aiden demanded.

"Cassie is missing," Nate said.

"Wait, what? How is that possible?"

"Officer Carrington, continue the search."

"Yes, sir."

Nate turned back to Aiden. "She hasn't been gone that long. It appears that she felt threatened, pulled the fire alarm and ran."

"She ran?" Aiden's voice pitched.

With a firm hand on his friend's shoulder, Nate said, "We'll start by searching the woods bordering the hospital. Knowing Cassie, if she was in danger she would have taken off, but perhaps didn't think it through to the end."

"She never does. She's so impulsive sometimes." Aiden's phone rang. He glanced at the screen. "It's Mom."

"We don't need more frantic people down here, Aiden. Let's focus on finding Cassie and then you'll call her back with good news, okay?"

Aiden nodded and paced a few steps away. "Hey, Mom. I have to call you back…in the middle of something. Soon, love you, bye." Aiden turned to Nate. "She knows something's up."

"Let's get to work. I've got a flashlight in my truck."

"Yeah, okay," Aiden said, dazed with worry about his sister. "I'll get mine, too."

Nate walked away, proud of himself for holding it together in front of his friend. He had no choice. As police chief, folks depended on him to be the grounding force in a crisis, and usually he excelled in that role.

Today was different. Someone was after Cassie. He never should have let her go to the hospital alone. He should have stayed with her, protected her. Right, and how ridiculous was that considering he had a potential murder on his hands?

He struggled to bury his concern and not let anyone see the utter panic tearing at his insides. But as he approached his truck, the bottled-up frustration got the better of him. He slammed his palm against the quarter panel.

A woman's cry echoed back at him.

Nate froze, his heart pounding.

Leaning forward, he peered into the flatbed. Cassie blinked her bloodshot, terrified eyes.

"You're in my truck," he said.

"D-d-disappointed?" She broke into a round of shivers.

He grabbed a blanket from the backseat and climbed into the flatbed beside her. As he gently covered her body, a wave of calm washed over him. She was okay. For now.

"Aiden!" He motioned to his friend who'd gone to get a flashlight. "Over here!"

"I knew you'd come."

Nate snapped his attention to Cassie. "What happened? Why did you run?"

"A guy…in the hospital…the guy with the shovel…from the cabin."

"Is it…?" Aiden stopped short and looked at her. "What are you doing in there?"

"Aiden," Nate warned, wanting him to soften his tone. "She's trembling."

"Let's take her inside," Aiden said.

"Nooooo." She clamped her hand around Nate's forearm. "Not back in there."

"Cassie, you need medical attention," Aiden argued.

"That man got to me in there. I can't go back." Her pleading blue eyes tugged at Nate's heart.

"She's delirious. She doesn't know what she's saying," Aiden said.

"I am n-n-not!" she protested.

"Come on, I'll help you out." Aiden reached for her.

"Wait," Nate said. "I've got another idea."

Cassie couldn't believe it. Nate had listened to her. He'd respected her fear of going back into the hospital and found an alternative.

Nate drove her to the urgent care, where Dr. Spencer was on duty. He was a good friend to both Nate and Aiden, and he'd done his share of triage with search and rescue. Cassie knew she wasn't suffering from anything serious, but she did need medical attention for the gash in her arm.

Closing her eyes, she relaxed under the heated blanket in the examining room. She appreciated the warmth that finally drove the chill from her bones.

"Cassie?"

She blinked her eyes open. A frown creased Nate's forehead.

"What's wrong?" she said.

"I thought you passed out."

"Why, because I stopped talking?" she joked.

Instead of smiling, he glanced down at his hands, holding his Echo Mountain PD cap. He seemed regretful, and she couldn't understand why.

"Thanks," she offered.

He looked at her. "For what?"

"Bringing me here. Listening to me, I guess. Not many people do that, especially not my brother."

"I almost forgot." He pulled her cell phone out of his jacket pocket. "Your cousin found it in the ambulance."

"Awesome, thanks. Where is my bossy brother, anyway?"

"He went outside to call your mom."

"Oh boy, now the whole town is going to know."

"Maybe that's not a bad thing," Nate said.

"You've got to be kidding."

"People will be on the lookout. They'll keep an eye on you."

"Right, because I'm so fragile and incapable of taking care of myself. They should consider the fact that I escaped this guy—" she hesitated "—twice, and the first time with a dog in my arms." She sat up. "Speaking of which, what happened to Dasher?"

"Relax, your sister and my sister are fighting over custody."

She sighed and lay back down. "Thanks, I'll pick him up after I get out of here."

"You should worry more about yourself than some scruffy dog."

"I have lots of people to support me, but Dasher? He's got no one. And besides, he's not scruffy, he's got character."

She thought Nate smiled but couldn't be sure.

The door slid open and Dr. Spencer poked his head into the room. "Sorry, had an emergency. I'll be back as soon as I can."

"Thanks," Cassie said.

Dr. Spencer smiled and shut the door. Cassie glanced at Nate. "When my brother comes back, you can go. I know you should be figuring out what happened to the dead woman, instead of hanging around here."

"Detective Vaughn is leading the investigation."

"Why?"

"I delegate in order to keep a broader perspective on things. I hope you don't mind me asking, but—" he pulled his stool close to Cassie's bedside "—do you think you can identify the man carrying the shovel?"

"Absolutely, and I wanted to call you with that information, but I'd lost my phone."

"I'll try to get a forensic artist to come by tomorrow. Where will you be staying?"

"You know where my apartment is, over the tea shop."

He straightened. "It would be wiser if you didn't go back to your place for a few days. The perpetrator knows who you are."

"I still don't understand how."

"Where's your wallet?"

"Back at the cabin. Oh…so you think he went through my things?"

"It's likely, yes."

"But I did a good job of playing a daft property manager who runs from the sight of blood. I was pretty convincing that I didn't see him at the cabin."

"Cassie, he came after you in the hospital and knocked out the orderly who was supposed to take you to imaging."

"Wait, what? Is he okay?"

"He's fine. That's not the point."

"I feel so bad since it's my fault that—"

"Cassie, stop talking, just for one minute."

She bit back more questions she wanted to ask about the injured orderly. At least she'd like his name so she could add him to her prayer list.

"We can't take chances with your safety," Nate said. "You need to be in the most protected environment possible until we solve this case."

"Well, I could always leave the country. I have enough money saved to travel for a while, not as long as I'd originally intended, but a few months should work, right?"

Nate didn't answer at first. He clenched his jaw and his green eyes darkened. "I'd rather you not."

"You said I'm in danger here, so the most logical choice is to—"

He stood abruptly. "You're a witness. I need you to stay in town."

"Oh, okay." She glanced at her fingers in her lap. Arguing with Nate was pointless. He was the police chief, after all, and his primary concern was the murder case, nothing more, nothing like…

He actually cared about Cassie.

Nope, Nathaniel Walsh was all business. He wanted to get his man, and Cassie was a means to that end.

"You're upset with me," he stated, studying her.

"I want to go home."

"To your mother's farm. Good idea."

She cocked her chin. "When did I say that? I never said that."

"But you agree that it's a good idea?" He sat back down beside her.

"No, I don't want to stay at the farm. Mom will hover and forbid me from leaving the house."

"It's probably a good idea to lie low for a while, stay at your mom's and do your blogging stuff."

"Hey, my blogging stuff doesn't pay the bills. I've made a commitment to Echo Mountain Rentals and it's good money."

"Right, it's about padding your getaway fund."

"You say that like it's a bad thing. You know what? Let's not talk about this. What do you need?"

"Excuse me?"

"What can your primary witness do to help you solve this case?"

"You're injured. I can conduct an interview tomorrow."

She continued anyway. "He was about six feet tall, with thin lips and bushy eyebrows. Oh, and a bump on his nose, here." She reached out to illustrate on Nate's nose, but he jerked away, like she was contagious.

"Wow, okay." She swallowed the hurt burning her throat and pointed to her own nose. "A bump right here. He's got dark brown eyes and he smelled of something… I can't put my finger on it, something pungent."

"What did he say to you?" Nate pulled a small notebook out of his jacket pocket.

"I did most of the talking. Especially after I figured out who he was. I did my best flaky girl impression, and told him I ran away from the cabin because of the blood, then tripped and fell down a mountain."

"You think he bought it?"

"He seemed to. I'm not dead." The inappropriate comment awkwardly slipped out.

Nate's fingers froze as he gripped the pen.

"Sorry, that was morbid," she said.

"Is there anything else you can tell me about him?"

"No, sorry."

He glanced up. "You have nothing to be sorry about."

In that moment she felt caught by something in his green eyes, something intense and sad. She struggled to form words.

"I… You… Thanks," she uttered.

She didn't like this feeling, a feeling of being derailed, yanked off course. It seemed to happen only when Chief Walsh was looking straight at her.

The door swung open. "How's the patient?" Dr. Spencer asked, approaching her.

His presence ripped Cassie out of the intense moment with the chief. She smiled at the doctor and said, "Pretty good, considering."

"Attitude is everything," the cheerful doctor said. "Let's stitch you up and send you home."

Nate stood. "I'll get her brother."

"Wait," she said. "Would you mind staying?" For some reason she didn't feel overly judged by Nate, whereas every word that came out of Aiden's mouth felt like a criticism.

"Are you sure?" Nate said.

"Yes, but you probably have to get back."

"I've got a few minutes." Nate offered to hold her hand for support.

She accepted the gesture, appreciating the warmth. As she focused on a spot across the room, the doctor raised the sleeve of her hospital gown and explained how he was numbing her arm in preparation for sutures.

A few minutes later she felt a tugging sensation, but no pain.

"Not so bad, right?" Dr. Spencer said.

She glanced at him. "That's it?"

"Only needed ten stitches. A little more paperwork and you're good to go." He smiled.

The sound of gunfire echoed through the door.

FOUR

Nate instinctively withdrew his firearm.

"Stay here," he said to Spence.

As Nate tried to pull away from Cassie, she clung tighter to his hand. Her face had drained of color.

"You're okay, Cassie, but I need to get out there and make sure everyone else is, too."

With a reluctant nod, she let him go, and he rushed to investigate.

"Be careful," she said.

He nodded, slid the door open and peered into the main area. It looked empty, as if staff had suddenly abandoned the urgent care. He left Cassie's examining room and shut the door.

Taking a few steps toward a computer station, he hesitated. Whimpering echoed from below. He knelt and peeked beneath a desk. Two staff members, young women in their twenties, were huddled together, fear coloring their eyes.

"Where did the shot come from?" he whispered.

One of the women pointed toward the reception area.

Just then the reception door flew open. Aiden and a middle-aged woman stepped into the examining area with their hands raised. Someone was obviously behind them. Nate took cover beside the desk to better assess what he was dealing with. If he exposed himself now he could lose his weapon in exchange for sparing someone's life. Without a weapon he had no control of the situation.

"She needs help now!" a male voice demanded. "Where's the doctor?"

"I—I don't know," the woman beside Aiden said.

"How can you not know?"

"Hey, can't we talk about this?" Aiden argued.

"Get down, facedown on the ground, and put your hands behind your head!"

Aiden must have hesitated, because another shot rang out and the two women beneath the desk shrieked.

"Okay, okay." Aiden dropped to the floor and made eye contact with Nate.

The assailant placed his boot on Aiden's back. "Now stay there. And you, get in a room!"

The front-end receptionist who'd entered with Aiden did as ordered.

If the guy would just move a few inches to the right Nate could get him from behind, the goal being to disarm him without the gun going off again.

"Where's the doctor? The nurses? I heard them scream."

The women under the desk eyed Nate. He shook his head, warning them off, not wanting to put more innocents in the line of fire.

The shooter turned. Nate saw the man's reflection in an examining room window: the shooter was holding on to a young, barely conscious woman.

"Nurses, get out here!"

Nate got ready to take his shot.

A door slid open. "I'm Dr. Spencer."

Nate froze. Spence was sacrificing his own safety to protect his patients and staff.

"What happened here?" Spence said calmly, as if the man wasn't threatening him with a gun.

"She's hurt, she's hurt and needs help and they said I had to wait for a doctor, but we can't wait!"

"I understand. Where is she hurt?"

As Spence engaged the shooter, Nate debated firing his weapon with so many innocents around. The last thing he wanted was to get into a heated exchange of gunfire.

He holstered his gun. The minute the perp's gun was no longer aimed at Spence, or anyone else for that matter, Nate would make his move. He'd take the guy down, hopefully before he could get a shot off.

"She's bleeding, can't you see that?" the guy said.

"I can't tell from this vantage point. How about we get her into a room?"

There were only three rooms: the receptionist was in one, an emergency patient in another, and Cassie in the third.

And hers was the closest.

"How did this happen?" Spence asked.

"Stop asking so many questions!" To drive home his point, the shooter pointed his weapon at the ceiling to fire off another shot.

Nate charged the guy from behind, the force making him release the injured woman. Distressed about letting her go, the guy lost his focus. Nate slammed the shooter's fist against the wall and the gun sprang free, dropping to the floor. Nate swung the guy to the ground, pinned him with a knee to his back and zip-tied his wrists.

"You've gotta help her," the man groaned.

Nate glanced at Aiden. "Help Dr. Spencer get the female victim into a room."

Aiden got up off the floor and assisted Spence.

"Ladies hiding beneath the desk?" Nate said.

Their heads popped out.

"Call 911. I need backup."

"I already did," Cassie said from the doorway of her examining room.

On cue, the wail of sirens echoed from the parking lot.

"You okay?" Nate asked Cassie.

"Yep."

Aiden approached Nate. "Doc says she'll need to be transported to the hospital. It's a gunshot wound."

"It was an accident," the perp said.

"You're under arrest for reckless conduct and aggravated assault," Nate said.

Red rushed into the examining area, gun drawn.

"Don't need the weapon." Nate stood, pulling the perp to his feet. "Take this guy to lockup."

"Yes, sir." Red led him away.

"Good job, Chief," Aiden said.

"Thanks." He glanced at Cassie. "Ready to go home?"

"Beyond ready."

"I'll take her to Mom's," Aiden offered.

"I don't think she wants to stay at the farm," Nate countered.

"It's okay. I'll go," Cassie said.

Nate guessed that after what just happened, she was upset and could use the support of family.

"But…" Cassie hesitated. "Can you drive me, Chief?"

"Come on, Cassie," Aiden said. "Nate has more important stuff to do."

"It's fine," Nate said. "I'll take her."

When she'd asked him to drive her to Mom's farm, she hadn't expected the chief to hang around as long as he did. He'd been here over an hour.

Mom, who lived alone since Dad's passing more than ten years ago, kept hammering him with questions about the dead woman, but he explained he couldn't discuss an ongoing investigation. She'd even bribed him with food, but he declined, opting for coffee instead.

He had a long night ahead of him. Not only had Cassie found a dead body, but then she wouldn't go back into the hospital, and ended up in the urgent care, where a man went nutty and shot up the place.

Her mom politely asked another question and Cassie jumped in for the save. "I think he needs a refill."

Mom glanced at his mug. "Oh, of course." She went into the kitchen to get the pot.

"I'm sorry," Cassie said to Nate.

Nate glanced up from his mug. "For what?"

"I feel like I'm a trouble magnet."

"I don't understand."

"The dead woman in the cabin, having to rescue me, Jesse James in the urgent care. You wouldn't have been there at all if not for my fear of the hospital."

"It was a good thing I *was* there or more people might have been seriously injured."

She shrugged. Her mind still spun about everything that had happened…and in one night!

"Here we go," her mom said, returning with the coffee. "We're so glad you could stay and chat for a bit. I'm sure it makes Cassie feel less anxious to have the chief of police here. It's important to keep her anxiety at a minimum."

"It's important to keep everyone's anxiety at a minimum," Cassie said.

"True, but we don't want yours triggering an episode."

Cassie shook her head, mortified. To have her illness mentioned in front of Nate made her feel broken and pitiful.

"Could I get some cream?" Nate asked Mom.

Not *what kind of episode*? Or *how bad is Cassie's issue with anxiety*?

Her big brother had probably told Nate the whole ugly story.

"Of course." Mom went back into the kitchen.

"I'm okay," Cassie said to Nate. "You don't have to stay."

"But your mom said—"

"I'm fine." She stood and paced to the front window. "I'm not going to freak out if you leave, and I haven't had an episode since I was a teenager."

"Oh, okay."

She turned to him. He was staring into his coffee.

"Go ahead, ask," she said.

He glanced up. "Ask what?"

"About my anxiety, my—" she made quote marks with her fingers "—episodes."

"It's none of my business."

"You mean Aiden hasn't told you?"

"No."

"I'm shocked. Well, you should probably know since everyone else seems to. I had a childhood autoimmune disease," she started, wandering back to the sofa. "Juvenile idiopathic arthritis. It's hard to diagnose in kids since there's no blood test for it. I'd be stiff in the morning, tired throughout the day, and not the most coordinated person on the planet. Aiden used to call me lazy bird. Since the symptoms would flare up and go away, it took a while to diagnose. Mom blames herself for not figuring it out sooner."

"Wasn't that the doctor's responsibility?"

"Sure, but she was the one who took care of me, saw me wince when I'd get up in the morning. I've outgrown it, but Mom can't see me as anything but that sick little girl."

"She loves you. It's her job to worry."

"But not her job to shame me in front of people."

"Shame you?"

"Telling you how my anxiety could trigger an episode? It's like I have no control over my health, but I do. I follow an anti-inflammatory diet and get my share of exercise."

"She might have some post-trauma issues related to your illness, Cassie. Try to see it from her point of view."

"Here we go," her mom said, breezing into the living room with cream for Nate's coffee. "Sorry it took so long, but I was looking for an appropriate accompaniment to the coffee. I know you said you weren't hungry, Chief, but I thought I'd tempt you anyway." She placed a tray of pastries on the coffee table and sat on the sofa beside Cassie. "So, what are we talking about?"

Nate's phone buzzed and he eyed the screen. "They need me." He glanced at Cassie as if waiting for her permission to leave.

Cassie stood and motioned toward the door. "Thanks for bringing me home."

"Wait," her mom said. "Let me put some sweets in a container to take with you."

Before he could respond, she'd dashed into the kitchen. Good old Mom, always feeding people to make them feel better.

"You'll be okay?" he asked Cassie.

"Yeah, don't worry about me. I'm tough."

The container of sweets on the seat beside him, Nate pulled away from the farmhouse. Glancing in the rearview, he couldn't ignore the pit in his stomach.

Don't worry about me.

Which was asking the impossible. Sure, the house had a new security system installed after the break-in last year, but the property was off the beaten path, and if Cassie and her mom needed emergency services it would take a good ten minutes to get to them.

A lot could happen in ten minutes.

Yet Nate couldn't be in two places at once. They might not have a large staff at the Echo Mountain PD, but SAR had its share of former military. Nate decided to see if Harvey, retired security manager for Echo Mountain Resort, could watch the farmhouse.

Harvey answered on the second ring. "Hey, Chief, heard you've had a busy night."

"Word gets around."

"How's Cassie McBride?"

"That's why I'm calling. She's staying at her mom's temporarily and I was wondering—"

"I'd love to."

"I haven't asked the question yet."

"You want me to keep an eye on Margaret and Cassie."

"If you've got time."

"Got plenty of that. Fishing trip was canceled so the timing is perfect. Besides, Margaret makes a dynamite cup of coffee."

"That she does. I'll let them know you're coming."

"Roger that."

Nate ended the call and pressed the speed dial for Cassie's cell phone. It rang a few times and went to voice mail. He fought the urge to turn the truck around and speed back to the farmhouse. He was overreacting. Cassie must be away from her phone, or maybe she'd gone to bed. She'd looked exhausted.

"Hi, this is Cassie. I can't take your call right now, but leave a message and I'll call you back. Have a blessed day." *Beep.*

"Cassie, it's Chief Walsh. I've asked Harvey to stop by and check on you and your mom. I didn't want you to be alarmed when he arrived." He hesitated, as if he wanted to say something else, something like everything was going to be fine, or how much he admired her for surviving a brutal childhood disease. "Okay, well, have a nice evening." He ended the call.

Maintaining his professionalism was key with Cassie McBride. Wasn't that why she called him Chief instead of Nate? It was a reminder to both of them that they didn't have a personal relationship. No matter how often she pestered him with questions for her blog, or seemed to show up whenever he was hurt on the job, Nate would never cross that line, a line his partner had crossed, which had cost him.

It could put her life in danger if Nate lost focus because of his attraction to Cassie.

His attraction to Cassie? Whoa, where had that come from? Well, who wouldn't be attracted to her? She was kind and engaging, independent and optimistic. Which made him wonder why she wasn't in a serious relationship.

When Nate asked Aiden about Cassie's social life, her brother said she blamed her family for scaring away suitors because they were so overprotective. Aiden countered that she was too picky—either that or she didn't want to get involved because of her travel plans. No one in Cassie's family approved of her taking off on her own to see the world. On one hand, Nate could understand why, yet he couldn't fault her for wanting to explore life outside of Echo Mountain.

Fifteen minutes later, Nate arrived at Whispering Pines cabin to check in with Detective Sara Vaughn. Before he went inside, he glanced at a text message from Cassie: Thanks for sending Harvey. Mom is excited for more company. ☺

Nate texted back: Glad to help. He hit Send and considered sending another text, something like *Have a good night* or *I'll see you in the morning.*

"I'm losin' it," he muttered and went into the cabin. He found Detective Vaughn conferring with a forensic specialist.

"Hey, Chief," she greeted.

The forensic officer retreated into the bathroom where they'd found the body.

"Initial cause of death looks like blunt force trauma, but there were no defensive wounds, no sign of a struggle, no evidence he restrained her. Nothin'." Her eyebrows furrowed. "So, what? She let him whack her head against the side of the tub? It makes no sense. We'll know more once they get her on the table."

"How about identification?"

"License reads Marilyn Brandenburg of Moscow, Idaho. We found an emergency number in her cell phone for a sister. I've called, but it keeps going to voice mail."

"Did you find Cassie McBride's purse on the premises?"

"There's a purple bag on the kitchen counter, why?"

"The killer came after her at the hospital. I'm trying to figure out how he knew who she was since she claims he didn't see her face."

"Wait, so she saw him, called for help and took off with a dog in her arms?"

"That is correct. I'm wondering if the perp took her wallet, which was how he identified her."

"I saw a wallet on the counter."

Nate went to the kitchen where Cassie's wallet, made from colorful duct tape, lay next to a bright purple bag. Cassie probably made the wallet herself, he mused. A few inches away he spotted a key chain with small charms: silver cross, flower, Union Jack flag, Eiffel Tower and kangaroo.

Fingering the keys made him wonder about the killer.

"Vaughn?" he called.

She popped her head out of the bedroom. "Sir?"

"Are we thinking the suspect escaped on foot? There were no cars in the area other than Cassie's."

"Someone spotted a black sedan at the Snoquamish trailhead. We're looking into it," Vaughn said.

"Good." He redirected his attention to Cassie's wallet.

He started to analyze the contents. Her round face smiled back at him from her driver's license. The killer would only have to glance at the license to determine Cassie's name and address.

Nate's fingers dug into the plastic wallet.

The address on her license was the farmhouse.

FIVE

Cassie tossed and turned in bed. Couldn't sleep. She hadn't spent the night at the farmhouse in months. Being back here, staying in her old room, brought back memories of a darker time, a time when she felt weak and helpless.

As she glanced out the window at a familiar tree, memories rushed back, bringing with them the irrational and paralyzing fear of being stuck in bed for the rest of her life.

She hopped out of bed, put her fleece on over her pajamas and grabbed her phone. A sip of water would stop this line of thinking. It always had in the past.

Heading toward the stairs, the sound of voices drifted from the first floor. Her mom and Harvey were talking in the living room.

Cassie hesitated at the top of the stairs.

"You should try and go back to sleep," Harvey said.

"I can't. I keep thinking about my daughter finding a dead body. She must be traumatized," her mom said.

"She's a tough cookie, Margaret."

"But she's not talking about it, at least not to me. I don't know what I ever did to put such distance between us. We were so close when she was a child."

Cassie gripped the cherrywood railing. If only she could articulate how her mom's overprotectiveness made Cassie feel like she couldn't breathe. But she struggled to find the right words. She'd never want to come off as disrespectful, and she'd certainly never want to hurt Mom's feelings.

"Kids go through awkward stages, then they grow out of it," Harvey offered.

"Yeah, when they're sixteen, not twenty-six," her mom answered. "I wish she would open up. I could help."

"Maybe she doesn't want to worry you."

"Too late for that."

A moment of silence, then, "How about some more coffee?" her mom offered.

"That would be great."

"And cookies?"

"If you got 'em."

"I always have cookies."

Cassie could just imagine the wry smile playing across her mother's lips. She was known as the "sweet queen," the woman who baked every day, always trying out a new recipe.

Too bad Cassie didn't inherit the baking gene. Her sister Bree seemed to get all the talent in that department.

Hearing her mom walk into the kitchen, Cassie decided to join Harvey in the living room. The sixtysomething former security manager, with a crewcut and kind blue eyes, had a grounding presence she appreciated. She went downstairs, and he looked up as she paused in the doorway.

"Couldn't sleep?" he asked.

She shook her head, entering the living room and flopping down in a chair.

"You've had quite the night," he offered.

"No kidding."

"You hanging in there?"

"Always do." She offered a smile.

Suddenly the lights went out, plunging them into darkness.

"Harvey?" Mom's concerned voice called.

He clicked on a small flashlight and pointed it toward the kitchen. "Probably the wind, Margaret. We're coming to you."

Just then his phone beeped with a text. The blue light illuminated his frown of concern as he read the message.

"What is it?" Cassie asked.

"Chief's on his way. The suspect might know this address." Harvey pulled a firearm out of his boot.

Panic stung the back of her throat. It wasn't only *her*

life being threatened, it was her mom's life, as well—the nurturing, compassionate matriarch of the McBride clan.

"Should we call 911?" Cassie asked Harvey.

"Chief took care of it. Let's get to your mom."

The nearly full moon lit the house through the sheer curtains covering the windows.

As Cassie and Harvey went into the kitchen, her heartbeat quickened. This was where they'd found Aiden, bloodied and semiconscious after the break-in last year. When Cassie glanced up and noticed the pale look on her mom's face, she shoved back the traumatic memory. She had to be strong.

"It's okay," Harvey said to her mom. "I'm not gonna let anything happen to you ladies."

The image of the dead woman in the Whispering Pines cabin flashed across Cassie's mind. Shovel Man had no problem killing or trying to kidnap a witness from a public place.

A red light blinked on the panel beside the back door. Someone had triggered the alarm.

It was a good thing the system was on a separate electrical circuit.

"He's…someone's trying to get in," her mom said in a terrified voice.

Cassie put a comforting arm around her. "It's okay. Police have been alerted and Harvey's here. We need to stay calm."

"Do you have a fire extinguisher?" Harvey said.

"Under the sink," Mom said.

"We can use it to stun him."

Cassie went to retrieve it. "Mom, get in the pantry."

"What about you?"

Cassie had no intention of hiding while Harvey fought off the intruder by himself.

"We both won't fit in there," she said. "I'll find another place." Gripping the extinguisher, she led Mom to the pantry.

"There's room for both of us," her mom whispered.

"Try to keep quiet," Cassie whispered.

"But—"

"Mom, please, I know what I'm doing." Cassie gently shoved her mom into the pantry, then shut and locked the door. She had to; she wouldn't risk Mom popping out during a dangerous encounter. Her parents had put the lock on the outside of the door, out of reach of the kids so they couldn't raid the cookie jar.

Cassie dreaded the lecture she'd get when this was over, but Mom was safe. That's what mattered.

Harvey nodded at an antique oak credenza beside the door leading to the living room. "Help me push this into the doorway."

It was a good plan, Cassie thought. By blocking the door between the kitchen and living room, the intruder could get to them only through the back of the house.

And they'd be ready.

The credenza firmly in place, Harvey motioned for Cassie to get on the opposite side of the back door, out of view. She crouched beside the kitchen cabinets, clutching the extinguisher to her chest.

"What if this is just a blown fuse?" she said.

"That'd be okay with me," Harvey answered. "But I don't believe in coincidences. You sure you won't go into the pantry with your mom?"

"I'm sure."

"Trying to prove how tough you are, huh?"

"Not proving anything. But I can take care of myself."

"I don't doubt that."

"Then you're the only one," Cassie said, noticing how their voices had grown softer in pitch as they spoke.

A few seconds of silence stretched between them. She thought she heard the echo of a police siren, but it was probably wishful thinking.

She glanced down at the vinyl flooring. Even in the dark-

ness, the moonlight illuminated a mark on the floor Aiden's
football cleats had made years ago.

A mark she had fixated on when he'd been attacked and
wounded last year.

"Hear that?" Harvey whispered.

Cassie took a deep, calming breath and focused.

Wooden boards creaked on the porch just outside the
kitchen. Someone approached the back door.

Please, God, give me courage.

Creak, creak…

The door handle rattled.

Cassie took another deep breath and removed the pin on
the extinguisher. A crash made her shoulders jerk. Mom really needed to replace the multipaned door.

Scratching echoed across the kitchen. The intruder was
trying to unlock the door, but that wasn't happening since
it was the kind you locked with a key from the inside.

Another crash echoed through the kitchen. The guy had
broken the window above the sink, probably in search of
another way inside.

"I know you're in there," he said. "Tell me what you did
with it and I'll leave you alone."

What she did with what?

Cursing under his breath, the intruder smashed all the
kitchen windows. Was he going to climb into the house?

Right above Cassie's hiding spot?

Harvey grabbed her, protectively shoving her behind
him.

Shovel Man popped his head through the window.

Harvey aimed his weapon. "I wouldn't."

The shrill sound of sirens echoed in the distance.

The guy retreated. Footsteps pounded across the porch.
She waited a good few minutes before speaking. "Think
he's gone?"

"Probably. But we'll stay here until help arrives."

The sirens grew louder, easing the tension in her shoulders.

And then the terrible sound of screeching brakes and crashing metal made her straighten. Cars must have collided on the farm road outside.

Chief's on his way, Harvey had said.

She jumped up and went to the window. "I can't see anything."

"Calm down," Harvey said.

She rushed to the pantry and opened the door.

"Listen, young lady—"

"The key to the back door, where is it?" she interrupted her mom.

"Above the phone."

Cassie dashed to the wall phone, grabbed the key and stuck it in the door.

"Hang on, Cassie," Harvey cautioned.

"There was a crash. People could be hurt." *Nate could be hurt.*

But she didn't say it. She couldn't.

"Cassie, you can't go running out there," her mom said.

Cassie whipped open the door and sprinted to the edge of the porch for a better look. She spotted a black sedan's grill buried in the side of the Chief's truck.

Harvey blocked her. "You need to wait until emergency shows up and we know it's safe."

She clasped her hands together, fighting the panic. The chief had to be okay. She whispered a prayer of hope, wondering how he had become so important in her life.

She was grateful to the chief, that's all. He'd saved her life more than once. Of course she'd be worried about his well-being.

Two squad cars peeled up the long dirt drive, followed by an ambulance. It felt like they took forever to approach the mangled cars.

Cassie squeezed her fingers tighter, fighting the urge to leap off the porch.

The patrol cars screeched to a halt, and the officers got out and drew their guns, aiming at the sedan.

"Okay?" she said to Harvey.

"Not yet."

She ached to see Nate open the passenger door, since the sedan had pinned the driver's door shut, and climb out of his truck. One of the officers pulled a guy out of the sedan and threw him to the ground.

Cassie took off. Mom called out to her, but Cassie didn't care. The threat was neutralized. As she got closer she recognized the driver—Shovel Man. Good. He was in custody. All was well.

Yet Nate hadn't opened his door.

She raced to the truck, spotted the white air bag, but couldn't see Nate's face, so she went to the passenger side and flung open the door.

She gasped at the blood smearing Nate's forehead and the side of his face. She would not fall apart like she had before.

"Nate?" she said, climbing into the front seat beside him.

Fingering the blood seeping down the side of his face, he glanced at her, confusion coloring his green eyes.

"Cassie?" he said, as if he wasn't sure he recognized her.

"You're okay," she said. She wasn't a doctor and couldn't be sure he was, in fact, okay, but figured he needed to be reassured out of his confused fog.

He studied her with a disoriented expression. Her pulse raced. Did he suffer a serious head injury?

She gripped his hand. "You're going to be just fine."

"Cassie, get out of the truck," her cousin Madeline said from behind her.

But Nate wouldn't let go of her hand. Cassie offered a gentle smile. "The paramedics need to clean your head wound. I'll be right out here."

With a nod, he released her, and she slid out of the truck. "He's conscious, but disoriented," she informed her cousin as she climbed into the front seat.

Cassie's eyes stung with unshed tears. Nate was a strong, healthy man, yet he seemed so vulnerable and lost.

She hovered beside the truck, hugging herself. Worrying, praying.

A gentle hand patted Cassie's back. She glanced sideways at her mom.

"He's a strong man," Mom said.

Cassie nodded, only then realizing she was in her pajamas, in public. And she didn't care.

"Here, I think this is yours," Madeline stuck out her hand, clutching Cassie's shoulder bag.

"Thanks." Cassie took it without looking inside the truck at the chief. It upset her too much to see him that way. Confused and broken.

Harvey joined Cassie and her mom. "Thanks for protecting us," Cassie said.

"My pleasure." He winked.

They waited.

A few minutes later, Madeline slid out of the truck, looking back at Nate. "Stay there until—"

"I'm coming out," Nate's angry voice argued.

"But we need to—"

"I'm fine."

Madeline shook her head in frustration and motioned for Rocky to bring the stretcher.

Nate shifted out of the truck, took one look at Cassie and said, "What are you doing out here?" He glanced at Harvey. "I told you to protect her."

Apparently the fog had lifted. No longer confused, the chief seemed steaming-hot mad.

"He did protect me," Cassie argued.

"You shouldn't have left the house."

"I had to make sure you were okay," she said, miffed that he was being so rude.

"Sorry to interrupt, but we need to take you to the hospital, Chief," Madeline said.

"Not necessary. What do I have to sign to release you from your responsibility?"

"Chief, you should get checked out," Cassie said. "You're bleeding."

"It's not serious."

"Okay, Dr. Walsh," she replied.

"He's right, it isn't serious," Madeline said. "But it wouldn't hurt to get checked out."

He motioned Madeline and Rocky away. "I'm fine. I need to make sure Cassie is safe."

"I'm safe. They arrested Shovel Man."

"We don't know if he's working alone." He glanced at Harvey. "Take Margaret to the resort. Since Aiden is the manager, he should be able to find her a secure room."

"Yes, sir." Harvey turned to Cassie's mom. "Let's pack some things and call your son."

"Cassie's coming with me, right?" Mom said.

The walls were closing in. Cassie loved Mom, but spending days upon days in a room with her, listening to her fret and worry over Cassie's health, would drive Cassie bonkers.

"I'd rather go back to my apartment," Cassie said.

"Honey—"

"That way if someone comes looking for me again, I'm not putting you in danger." She gave her mom a hug, glancing into Chief Walsh's eyes.

He studied her, as if trying to figure out what was going on in her mind. She looked away, her gaze landing on the inside of his truck, the deflated air bag. He could have been seriously hurt.

Because of her.

"We'd better get going," Chief Walsh said. "I'll protect Cassie.

She broke the hug with Mom and said, "Keep your phone on and I'll text you."

"Be safe."

"I will. Promise."

Harvey led her mom back to the farmhouse. This was the best plan for so many reasons. She turned to Nate and caught him rubbing his forehead.

She touched his arm. "Does your head hurt? I'll get my cousin."

"Not necessary. I'm just trying to figure out how everything fits together, that's all."

"That's a lot. Maybe you should wait until you've had a good night's sleep."

Sleep wasn't in the plan for Nate, not anytime soon. Not until he could be sure Cassie was safe.

Since his truck had been damaged, he'd driven Cassie to her apartment in a squad car, and remained outside her building all night. Nate had an officer patrol the area to make sure it was safe, that no one was lurking and waiting for an opportunity to strike.

Although that scenario seemed unlikely, he wasn't taking any chances. Since Cassie hadn't bothered to change her address on her driver's license, it would be difficult for someone to track her down. He wished he would have known about her not changing her address on her license before she let him take her to the farmhouse. Maybe it had slipped her mind, or maybe she was in denial that the perp would come after her again.

Nate doubted anyone had tracked her to the quaint, modest apartment, but couldn't be too careful. This case grew more complicated by the hour.

The next afternoon, he spotted Cassie waving to him from her window. Nate went up to her apartment to discuss the case.

"You've been down there all this time?" she asked from the kitchen.

"One of my officers gave me a break."

He peered through the delicate lace curtains in her living room, scanning the street below. It wouldn't be easy to breach her apartment considering the two entry doors downstairs, plus Cassie's apartment door. She lived in an older building with a mailbox vestibule, and her mailbox, 2D, did not have her name on it, which worked in their favor.

"Shouldn't you be interrogating Shovel Man?" she said, coming into the living room carrying a tray with a teapot and cups.

"Shovel Man?" He raised an eyebrow.

"I didn't know what else to call him."

"He's still at the hospital being treated for injuries sustained in the collision. I'll question him in lockup after he's discharged."

"How about some tea?" she asked, pouring herself a cup.

"You don't have to entertain me. Just pretend I'm not here."

If only Nate could follow his own advice. It was impossible to ignore the intimacy of being surrounded by Cassie's personal things, wall posters of castles and mountains overseas, and family pictures proudly displayed on oak bookshelves.

"I can't believe I slept until midafternoon."

"You obviously needed it."

"Why not sit down and take a breath?" She shifted onto the sofa.

He decided this could be a good opportunity to question her about the events of last night to help with the investigation.

Stop being so insensitive. The woman is probably still traumatized from surviving violent encounters with a criminal.

Yet the sooner he got answers, the safer she'd be.

"Tell me again what the intruder at the farm said."

Cassie poured him a cup of tea. "That if I'd tell him what I did with—" she made quotes with her fingers "—'it,' he'd leave me alone."

"Did with what?"

"Wish I knew." She handed him a delicate china cup.

He took it, noting how fragile it felt in his large hands. "Did you take anything from the cabin, other than the dog?"

"No." Her eyes widened. "You don't think they're after Dasher, do you? Why would anyone be after a dog? Speaking of which, is he okay? Who's got him? Catherine or Bree? Did Bree take him to the vet to get checked out?"

Nate cracked a smile.

"What?" she challenged.

"I can tell you're back to normal because you're firing off ten questions at once." He sat on the sofa beside her.

"Oh, sorry."

"Don't be. I'm glad you're okay. Dasher is safe with your sister. Apparently he and your sister's dog are hitting it off. They didn't take him to the vet because he didn't suffer any physical injuries."

"Speaking of which, hang on." She got up and went into the kitchen.

Nate glanced at his watch. He hoped the perp would be released from the hospital and taken back to the station soon, but Nate didn't want to leave Cassie alone just yet.

He'd left her alone last night and couldn't forgive himself for the trouble that followed.

She breezed back into the living room holding an ice bag. It amazed him that she had so much energy considering everything that happened to her yesterday.

"Here." She sat down and held the ice against his head. "To reduce the swelling. Still looks pretty red from last night."

"Thanks." He reached up and his fingers brushed against her hand.

Her skin was so warm and soft, and his breath caught in his throat. What was happening to him? He wasn't a teenager, and he'd certainly outgrown the crush stage of relationships. Why did this woman rattle him so?

"I've got it, thanks," he said.

"Oh, sure, right." She snapped her hand away and reached for her teacup. "My mother's overprotective instincts must be rubbing off on me. Sorry."

"Cassie?"

She glanced up at him with those iridescent blue eyes.

"You never need to apologize to me, okay?" he said.

She bit back a smile. "Even if I do something nasty?"

"Define nasty," he said, surprised by their sudden light-hearted banter.

"Hmmm, what if I doused your tea with happy herbs like lemon balm or chamomile?"

He glanced into his cup. "I probably deserve that."

"I'm kidding," she said. "Stop being so serious."

The lightness of the moment destroyed by his dark thoughts, he slid his cup onto the table.

"My seriousness will keep you safe." He stood and went to look out the window. "I can't afford to be distracted by tea and conversation."

Man, he sounded like a jerk.

"I get it, I do." She got up and crossed the room.

He felt her hand touch his back. Warmth spread across his shoulders. She had that kind of effect on him—a peaceful, calming effect.

"But I think that instead of getting pulled down by the darkness, we should focus on strategizing our way out of this mess."

When she put it like that it made him seem like an unprofessional, emotional head case.

"Are you worried about how all this will reflect on your position as chief?" she asked.

He turned to her, wanting to read her expression. It was authentic and open. Her eyes always seemed so honest when she looked at him.

Which meant she honestly thought he was more worried about his job than her safety. She hadn't a clue how he felt, that this wasn't just about protecting a random citizen.

No, this couldn't happen. These feelings could get her killed. He went to the coffee table to get his teacup.

"Or is it something else?" she pushed.

"I don't want to mess up."

"No one does," she said.

He turned to her. "People died because I wasn't paying enough attention." How had that slipped out?

"I'm so sorry."

"Yeah, well, you can't fix the past."

"No, but you can let it go."

"Wish I could." He sighed. "And now, well, Echo Mountain has historically been a quiet town, until recently."

"Until what, you came on board as chief? Don't even go there, big guy. We had our share of trouble long before you took over, like the guys stalking Scott, and the thugs after Nia because of her deadbeat brother. And now I find a dead body. I'm sorry it was on your watch."

"Wait, you're not blaming yourself for this," Nate said.

"No, but I feel responsible for putting the people I care about in danger."

She glanced at him with a startled expression, like she'd blurted out a secret she hadn't meant to share. Awkward tension filled the living room.

"Don't worry, your mom will be fine." Nate recovered. "Aiden will make sure of it."

She nodded, but didn't speak.

I feel responsible for putting the people I care about in danger.

Her words hung in the air between them, and Nate considered their meaning. She couldn't possibly include him on that list.

He had to redirect his thinking before it totally distracted him from his goal: protecting Cassie and finding out why "Shovel Man" killed the woman in the cabin.

"To be clear, you didn't take anything from the rental cabin?" he said.

"Just the dog," she said, breaking eye contact and walking back to the sofa.

"What were you supposed to do when you got there?"

"Check appliances, general condition of the cabin, bring in fresh toiletries and linen. But I didn't get very far because I heard Dasher scratching at the closet door." She shook her head. "I wasn't even supposed to be there."

"Explain, please."

"My friend Becca had originally been assigned the Whispering Pines cabin, but I offered to cover for her. She seemed stressed lately."

"Why's that?" Instead of sitting beside her, he chose a chair across from the coffee table.

"I think she's having boyfriend trouble. Tony keeps promising to get a better job. He does part-time work for Echo Mountain Rentals and she's been supporting them by holding down two jobs."

He pulled out his notebook. "I need Becca and Tony's last names."

"Wait, why? You think they're involved in this?"

He glanced up at her trusting and offended expression. "She might have seen or heard something along the way," he said. "I have to look into everything connected to the rental company. Detective Vaughn has already been in touch with your boss."

"Oh, okay."

Cassie gave him Becca's last name and her phone number. "I don't know Tony's, sorry."

He looked at her with a raised eyebrow.

"Oh, right, I'm not supposed to say 'sorry.' Sorry." She smiled.

He refocused on his notebook to avoid the effect her disconcerting smile was having on him.

"I'll call it in." He pulled his phone off his belt.

He called Detective Vaughn and gave her the information about Becca and Tony.

"You think they're tied to the deceased?" Vaughn said.

"I have no idea," he said into the phone. "Cassie said Becca has been stressed out. It's worth looking into."

"I'm on it."

"And let me know when the suspect is in lockup."

"Of course."

He ended the call and turned to Cassie. "We'll figure this out."

An explosion echoed through the windows. Cassie shrieked and Nate instinctively pulled her against his chest.

SIX

Cassie had never heard anything so ear-piercingly loud, yet the eerie silence that followed was even creepier.

She felt guilty about clinging to Nate like a little kid, and knew she should let go. Yet he'd been the one to reach for her. It wasn't like she'd jumped into his comforting arms that held her snugly against his chest. The pressure of their embrace dissolved the ball of fear lodged in her throat.

Then she realized Nate couldn't investigate what was going on outside with Cassie stuck to him like Velcro.

Releasing him, she stepped back. "I'm okay."

"You're sure?"

"Yes, go ahead. Do your thing."

He called it in. "This is Chief Walsh. There's been an explosion on Main Street. I can't tell what it is or from where it originated. Send a patrol car and I'll meet him in front of the Sweet Rose Teashop." He pocketed his phone and looked deep into Cassie's eyes. "I need you to stay here and lock the door behind me. Don't let anyone in but me, got it?"

"Of course," she said with false confidence. He must have read fear in her eyes because he didn't move.

"Go, go." She led him to the door and securely locked it once he left.

She stood there for a good minute, pressing her forehead against the aged wood, praying that Nate wouldn't be harmed and he'd return quickly.

"Uh," she moaned, going back to the sofa and grabbing her cup. Five minutes, she wanted five peaceful minutes to ground herself from the craziness.

Then she realized she *had* felt grounded the moment Nate pulled her into his arms. Wow, that was a first. She'd dated a few guys, sure, but she'd never felt calmed by any of them. Considering the current situation—being stalked and threatened—it was quite remarkable that she could feel grounded from a simple hug.

"Of course he makes you feel safe. He's the police chief," she said.

As the minutes ticked by, she grew more anxious about what was happening outside, wondering if Nate was okay. She padded to the living room window and peered down to the street. A cruiser with flashing lights was parked in front of her building, but there was no sign of Nate or the other officer.

"Where are you?" she whispered.

A sudden movement caught her eye. On the corner, she noticed a man standing under a streetlamp, lighting a cigarette.

And he was staring up at her.

She snapped back from the window, her heart racing. Now she was overreacting about everything. She wasn't in danger. Shovel Man was in custody. The guy outside was probably out for a walk and happened to pause at the corner to light a cigarette.

As she was about to peek outside again, someone knocked on her apartment door. She gasped. How did they get into her building?

She slowly crossed the room and eyed the peephole. The hallway was empty. Taking a few steps away from the door, she whipped out her phone to text Nate.

"Cassie, open up!" her sister called.

Cassie eyed the peephole again. Bree stood there holding Dasher in her arms. Cassie flung open the door.

"How did you get in my building?"

"Key, remember?" Bree waved her key chain. "You going to let me in?"

Cassie motioned her inside.

"Mom wanted me to check on you," Bree said, carrying the dog in one hand and a take-out bag in the other. "She told me to bring food."

"Hey, Dasher." Cassie grabbed him for a quick hug.

"Mom told me what happened. You seriously locked her in the pantry?"

"It seemed like a good idea at the time." Cassie shrugged. "Thanks for bringing Dasher, and dinner."

"I figured you could use the company."

"I had company until a few minutes ago. Didn't you see the police car out front?"

"I parked in back."

"Chief Walsh was here."

Bree quirked an eyebrow.

"Knock it off," Cassie said. "He's just doing his job."

Bree's phone beeped. She held it up. "Mom."

"Go ahead, tell her I'm okay."

Bree answered. "Hi Mom…Yeah, I'm with her now. She's okay…I'll tell her. Love you, too." Bree pocketed her phone. "Mom says she loves you even if you won't stay with her at the resort."

"It's safer for Mom this way."

"I wish you would've called me instead of me having to hear about it from Mom," she said in her hurt voice.

Bree had survived her share of violent situations, and Cassie wanted to spare her big sister more trauma.

"Cassie?" Bree prompted.

Cassie put Dasher down and watched him enjoy all the new smells of her apartment. "I'm okay…well, I was okay until we heard an explosion outside just now. Chief Walsh went to investigate. He said not to open the door to anyone but him and when you knocked, I couldn't see you through the peephole."

"I was picking up the dog, sorry. What is going on around here? First the body in the cabin, then a crazy man in urgent care, and someone tried to break into the farmhouse? How are you coping with all this?"

"I'm fine." Cassie glanced at the window across the room. "I just wish Chief Walsh would let me know he's okay."

"Want me to look?" Bree started for the window.

"No, stay away from the window."

"What? Why?" Bree studied her.

"I saw a guy out there. It's probably nothing."

"Honey." Her sister took Cassie's hand. "Never, ever ignore your instincts. If you think there was something off about the man outside, then respect that feeling."

Bree knew a lot about trusting her instincts. She'd learned the hard way after surviving a relationship with an abusive boyfriend. She'd also found a wounded man in the mountains named Scott, and trusted her instincts that told her he was not a criminal. Scott turned out to be a wonderful man who was now Bree's boyfriend.

"We'll tell Nate about the strange man outside," Bree said.

"No." Cassie pulled her hand away. "I'm probably overreacting."

"Or maybe not. Why don't you want to tell him?"

Cassie sat on the sofa and Dasher jumped up beside her. "Nate's got enough going on. He doesn't need to deal with my paranoia about some phantom stranger."

"That's not it," Bree challenged, joining her on the sofa. "Come on, out with it."

"Look, he already thinks of me as his friend's bubble-headed little sister who talks way too much. Why add overreacting, hysterical woman to that list? I don't want him looking at me that way. I want him to see me as…" Her voice trailed off as she noticed a wry smile playing across her sister's lips. "What?" Cassie challenged.

"Nothing." Bree winked.

"What's with the wink?"

"Admit it, his opinion of you means so much because you kinda like him."

"He's the police chief. Everyone likes him."

"I'm not talking *that* kind of like. I'm talking hugging and holding hands and—"

"Stop." Cassie stood, grabbed the food bag and went

into the kitchen. She had to get away from her sister's teasing comments.

More like, unavoidable truth.

Drat, who was Cassie kidding? She'd been crushing on Nate Walsh for months and kept pushing it away, telling herself he'd never be interested in a naive chatterbox like her.

She also knew he was the exact *wrong* person to date because of his dedication to his job. She wanted to take off and explore the world, whereas Nate was firmly rooted in the community as police chief. He wasn't going anywhere anytime soon.

"Cassie?" her sister said from the kitchen doorway. "I understand if you don't want to admit it to me, but at least be honest with yourself."

Cassie glanced at her sister. "Nate is not an option."

"Why not?"

"I can't stay here, Bree. I need to get out of this town."

"Okay, well, make sure you're running toward your dreams, not fleeing your problems."

The apartment buzzer went off. Cassie pressed the intercom. "Hello?"

"It's Nate."

"Come on up." She pressed the unlock button. A minute later she spotted his handsome face in the peephole. She opened the door and the dog burst into furious barks.

"Stop, Dasher, it's Chief Walsh." Cassie picked up Dasher and glanced into Nate's eyes. "What was the explosion?"

"Someone started a Dumpster fire behind the hardware store. Probably kids needing a little excitement." He glanced at Bree. "Hi, Bree."

"Chief."

He studied Cassie, cocking his head slightly. "What's wrong?"

"What? I… What do you mean what's wrong?" Cassie stumbled.

"Did something happen while I was gone?"

Cassie glanced at Bree, who bit back a knowing smile. Nate could read Cassie like a three-word text.

"Everything's fine," Cassie said, going to the sofa.

"She saw a suspicious guy outside and it freaked her out."

"Bree!" Cassie snapped.

"Where?" Nate said.

"By the lamppost on the corner," Cassie said. "It was probably nothing."

"Stop denying those instincts," Bree repeated.

"Good advice." Nate went to the window. "No one's there now. What did he look like?"

"Tall, wearing a baseball cap and smoking a cigarette."

"She's pretty jumpy," Bree added.

"You can leave now," Cassie said, half-joking.

"I don't want to leave you alone."

"She won't be alone," Nate said. "I'm staying for a while."

"Good, well, there's plenty of food for both of you."

"Guys, I can take care of myself," Cassie said, putting Dasher down.

"Bree, how about I escort you to your car," Nate offered, and then looked at Cassie. "I'll be right back."

"Hey, don't I get a say in any of this?" Cassie protested.

Bree hugged her. "Don't argue. Enjoy his company," she whispered in her ear.

"Stop." Cassie playfully shoved at her sister's shoulder. "Did you want to keep the dog?"

"You should probably take him until all this is sorted out. He'll have more fun at your place with Fiona, anyway."

Bree picked up the dog and smiled. "Have a nice evening."

Cassie's cheeks must have reddened, because Bree darted into the hallway. Seemingly unaware of Cassie's embarrassment, Nate followed Bree, and Cassie locked the door behind him.

Nate escorted Breanna safely to her car, then decided to walk the block to see if the suspicious-looking man Cassie had noticed was still hanging around. Other than the fire department making sure the Dumpster fire was out, Main Street was relatively quiet. There was no sign of the guy.

As he made his way back to Cassie's apartment, his phone vibrated. He pulled it off his belt. It was his mentor, former Police Chief Washburn.

"Chief," Nate said.

"Heard you've had a busy twenty-four hours."

"Nothing I can't handle."

"That's what I've been saying."

Nate hesitated outside Cassie's apartment building. "Have you been getting calls?"

"Just one or two."

Which probably meant half a dozen, but the chief didn't want to worry Nate.

"Do I need to hold a press conference?" Nate half joked.

"Nothing that public. But be willing to talk to people if they ask questions. It's not every day a dead body shows up in town."

"I get it, I do, but my primary focus has to be solving the case."

"I hear frustration in your voice. If there's anything I can do to help, I'm here, trying to enjoy retirement, and failing miserably, by the way."

"Thanks. I might take you up on that offer. You're around this week?"

"Around with a honey-do list in hand. Nothing that can't wait. I'm serious, son, call if you need anything."

"Will do. Have a good night."

"You, too. And Nate?"

"Sir?"

"I recommended you for the job because I have one hundred and twenty percent confidence in your abilities."

"Thank you, sir." Nate ended the call.

What did Nate have to do to convince the townsfolk that

he was a solid choice for chief, that he could protect them as well as Chief Washburn had for the past twenty years?

He went to Cassie's building and she buzzed him in. Once upstairs, he spotted her peering through a crack in her apartment door.

"You took longer than I thought." She motioned him inside.

"Got a call from Chief Washburn."

"Everything okay?"

"As long as I solve this case by tomorrow, sure."

"People have been calling him?" She sat down on the sofa.

"How'd you guess?"

"I've lived in this town for twenty-six years, remember? People worry when they hear things and don't know what's going on. It's not a personal reflection on you or anything."

"Thanks."

"No, thank you for taking Bree to her car. You should have let her stay so you wouldn't have to."

"It's my job."

An odd, almost pained expression flashed across her face. She motioned to the TV.

"I was watching television, unless you'd prefer quiet."

"Television's fine."

It didn't surprise him that the station was tuned to a travel show.

He sat down on the sofa, a safe distance away from her. "So, Ireland, huh?" he said, nodding at the screen.

"England, France, Switzerland and eventually Australia, although that's a superlong flight. I'd need tons of plane activities to get me through that one."

"Plane activities?"

"Sure, movies, puzzles, books, you know, activities."

He couldn't help but smile. This woman fascinated him on so many levels, especially her enthusiasm for life and new experiences.

"You're smiling," she said. "It's a good look on you," she teased.

Again, as they drifted into natural conversation, he warned himself not to get too comfortable. "Other than the challenges of living in a small town, why are you so desperate to travel?" he asked.

"It's a long story."

"I'm not going anywhere for a while, remember?"

She shrugged. "I made myself a promise when I was a kid. As I lay in bed, praying my body would finally work the way it was supposed to, I promised myself that when I recovered I would visit all the places I read about in books. I would climb mountains and watch the Eiffel Tower light up on New Year's. Too bad I hadn't left last week, huh? That would have made my life so much simpler."

He didn't have a response for that, realizing how much he'd miss her once she left. "I'll figure this out, Cassie," he said, hoping to ease her fears. "I promise."

A few hours later, after a pleasant meal courtesy of her sister, Nate found himself on the sofa beside Cassie as she watched another travel program. His phone vibrated with an incoming call. It was Detective Vaughn. He started to get up.

"It's okay. You can take it here," she said, turning down the volume on the TV.

He sensed she wanted him to stay close, so he leaned against the sofa and answered the call. "Detective?"

"The perp's license reads Len Pragner of Chicago. Someone saw him check into the Rushing River B&B, alone. I haven't been able to question him. His injuries were worse than we thought, so he's still at the hospital. Want me to stay?"

"No, see if Carrington can cover for a few hours so you can get some sleep."

"Copy that. The deceased has been transported to the ME's office."

"Good. I'll be posted outside Cassie McBride's apartment

tonight. I can't risk her being alone, not until we figure out why someone's after her."

Nate felt pressure on his arm and glanced down. Cassie had fallen asleep against his shoulder.

"Any idea why she's been targeted?"

"When the suspect stuck his head through the kitchen window he said if she told him where *it* was, he'd leave her alone. They want something from her, but the only thing she took from the cabin was the dog."

"Strange," Vaughn said.

"Have you found any connection between Pragner and our vic, Marilyn Brandenburg?"

"Not yet. I'll do a more thorough check tomorrow when I get to the station."

"Good night, Detective." He ended the call and glanced at the blond-haired beauty leaning against him. He shifted to get up, but she was gripping his sleeve, mumbling something he couldn't make out. She'd fallen asleep, and found comfort clinging to Nate's jacket. He didn't have the heart to wake her up.

As he puzzled through tonight's events, his gaze drifted to the television program. The travel show reminded him that this, the feel of Cassie leaning against him and depending on him for comfort, was temporary. Still…there was no harm in enjoying the moment.

The next morning Cassie awoke up with a start, anxious and disoriented. She opened her eyes and focused on her antique nightstand lamp. She was in her bedroom, on her bed. Sitting up, she realized she was on top of the comforter with a blanket tucked snugly around her body.

"Nate?" she said, her voice hoarse.

Footsteps echoed down the hallway. Her heartbeat quickened.

Her brother stepped into the doorway holding a white

to-go cup from the tea shop below. "Good morning, sunshine."

"Where's Chief Walsh?"

"At work. What did you think, he was going to be your personal bodyguard for the rest of the week?" Aiden motioned to his cup. "Got you some coffee." He disappeared from the doorway.

"Coffee, bleh," she muttered under her breath, and flopped down against the comforter.

The last thing she remembered was leaning against Nate on the sofa while watching television. She must have fallen into a deep sleep and he'd carried her to her room. She wished he'd stayed long enough for her to tell him...tell him what? Well, at least long enough to thank him again for protecting her.

"That's unacceptable," Aiden's voice drifted down the hall. "We need the heating system repaired by the weekend. We'll be at seventy-five percent capacity."

Cassie felt like such a burden, taking Aiden away from his managerial responsibilities at the resort, and Nate away from his police chief duties.

She felt like that little kid again, trailing behind her older siblings who cast irritated smirks over their shoulders at her. She was the afterthought, holding everybody back, dragging everyone down with her problems...her ill health.

Determined not to be that needy child, she shifted out of bed, appreciative that she'd outgrown the morning stiffness of her childhood illness. Today she was a healthy and independent woman. She must be out of danger if Nate left her apartment, right?

Heading into the living room, she waved Aiden down as he paced. "I'm going to take a quick shower and go to work," she said.

He held the phone against his flannel shirt. "What are you talking about?"

"I have to stop by the rental office and turn in my report on the properties. I'm a day late as it is."

"I'll call you back," he said into the phone. He shot Cassie a stern frown. "Email or call it in."

"Mr. Anderson doesn't do email reports, Aiden."

Aiden shook his head. "How does that guy stay in business?"

"Besides, I need to go in person and explain what happened."

"Oh, I'm sure they know."

"It's my job, Aiden."

"Don't you remember what happened over the past thirty-six hours?" he said in that condescending tone of his.

"I remember," she shot back. "I also remember the suspect was taken into custody."

"Why can't you—"

"I won't stay locked away like a caged bird. I need to get out of here and live my life." Cassie realized the words came out a little stronger than she'd intended, but she was desperate to get through to her brother.

He studied her for a second. "Fine. I'll take you to the resort. I had your car towed there this morning. Maybe Mom can change your mind."

He whipped out his phone and continued his argument with the repair company.

An hour later they arrived at the resort where she checked on her mom, who was set up in a nice room facing the grounds.

"I was so worried about you," Mom said, hugging Cassie.

"Thanks, I'm okay. Looks like you're okay, too."

"My son takes good care of me." She smiled at Aiden.

"Well, I'm off to the rental office," Cassie said.

"Cassie, no, you—"

"It's fine, Mom. They've got the suspect in custody."

"Honey, you shouldn't be gallivanting around town on your own," her mom said.

"She won't listen," Aiden said, checking text messages.

Cassie clenched her jaw to quell the protest threatening to crawl up her throat and burst out of her mouth.

"I'll be fine," she said.

"Aiden, go with her," Mom said.

Aiden's beeper went off.

"Mom, he's got a work crisis. I'll be back in an hour."

She gave Mom a hug and turned to leave, but Mom was determined to walk her to her car. Cassie felt Mom's silent guilt trip, even though she didn't speak.

"Cassie, I—"

"Love you," Cassie interrupted and kissed her on the cheek.

She got behind the wheel of Ruby and spotted the manila envelope in the passenger seat containing completed reports from the other cabins she'd visited.

As she drove away from the resort, the swell of frustration loosened around her throat. This was why she needed to build her travel fund and get out of town. She loved her mom and siblings but felt smothered and didn't know how to communicate her frustration.

She avoided glancing in the rearview mirror, not wanting to see her mother's worried expression, the one that still haunted Cassie from childhood.

The expression that reminded her how broken she was.

Was, but not anymore.

Make sure you're running toward your dreams, not fleeing your problems. Bree's comment taunted Cassie.

"I'm not running away, I'm not," she said.

Fearing she wasn't being completely honest with herself, Cassie flipped on the radio as a distraction and found a country station. Lyrics about sacrifice in the name of love filled the car.

She clicked it off. She wasn't going to give up her dream

of traveling in order to make her family happy, no matter how much she loved them. Nor should they expect it.

As far as romantic love was concerned, Cassie had plenty of time for that later, after she'd seen the world. Who knows, maybe she'd even find the love of her life overseas and decide to relocate to Europe. Wouldn't that fry everyone's fritters?

"Oh, grow up," she scolded herself, realizing how juvenile she sounded. Yet sometimes the way they hovered made her feel like the walls were closing in, and she couldn't breathe.

A few minutes later she pulled into the parking lot of Echo Mountain Rentals. She got out of her car, preparing to apologize for being late with her incomplete report. As she approached the entrance, she noticed the front door was ajar.

Just as it had been at the Whispering Pines cabin.

The hair prickled on the back of her neck.

Never, ever ignore your instincts.

She scanned the parking lot and noted only one other car, not her boss's. She darted out of sight, her back hugging the side of the building, and called Nate.

"This is Chief Walsh. Please leave a message and I'll call you back. If this is an emergency call 911."

Cassie texted him instead: SOS @ EM Rental office. Front door open. Danger?

She sent the text. But if he was in a meeting or interrogating Shovel Man, he wouldn't be able to respond immediately.

Never, ever ignore your instincts.

Cassie debated.

A crash echoed from inside the office.

She dialed 911.

"911. What is your emergency?"

"I'm at the Echo Mountain Rentals office," she whispered. "I think someone's breaking in."

"What's your name?"

"Cassie McBride."

"Why do you think someone is breaking in?"

"The front door is open and my boss's car isn't here and I heard a crash."

She glanced up.

A tall man wearing jeans, black boots and a black jacket crossed the parking lot and approached Cassie's car.

He slid his hand into the inside of his jacket.

And pulled out a gun.

SEVEN

Nate stood at the foot of the perpetrator's hospital bed and considered his next move. Len Pragner seemed to be enjoying this—Nate asking questions; Len not answering. A half smirk curled the guy's lips like he had a secret, like he thought the handcuffs were going to magically open and he'd walk out of the hospital, all charges dropped.

"We've got you on attempted assault, breaking and entering—"

"I didn't enter," Len said.

"Because someone was pointing a gun at your head."

"And I didn't assault anyone," he argued.

"You smashed the windows and tried getting into the farmhouse. That'll keep you in town for a while."

Len shrugged. "It's a nice town. Friendly people."

"My witness says you were looking for something."

"Your witness, you mean Cassie McBride?"

"What were you looking for?"

"She's cute, not my type, but cute."

Nate struggled to keep his temper in check. "Why are you in Echo Mountain?"

"I think I might ask her out," he taunted.

Nate narrowed his eyes, but kept his cool. Len couldn't possibly know how Nate felt about Cassie.

"You keep playing games, Len," Nate said. "We've got a nice cell waiting for you when you're released."

Nate left the guy's room and motioned to his officer on duty. "When the doctor releases him, he goes straight to lockup."

"Yes, Chief."

Detective Sara Vaughn approached Nate. "From the look on your face I'm thinking he isn't being cooperative."

"He's enjoying pushing me around. Feel free to give

it a try." He glanced at his phone. A text popped onto the screen from Cassie.

An SOS.

"I've gotta go." Nate rushed to the stairs, made it to his squad car and took off. As he listened to the radio chatter, he heard an officer responding to a B&E call at the Echo Mountain Rentals office.

She shouldn't have left her apartment; then again, the suspect was in custody, so she didn't seem to be in immediate danger.

Unless Len had a partner. The man standing on her street corner, perhaps?

Nate pressed down on the accelerator, struggling to quiet the shame coursing through his mind: *You never should have left her.*

Yeah, and how unrealistic was that? He was the police chief; he had a job to do, a homicide to solve.

A town to keep safe.

He turned into the rental company parking lot and spotted Cassie's red car, a black sedan, and a patrol car, lights flashing. He didn't see anyone in cuffs. Nate approached his officer, who stood beside his car speaking with a taller gentleman in his forties.

"Officer Hough?"

Officer Hough turned to Nate. "A misunderstanding, Chief. The caller thought this man was a burglar, but he's with the FBI."

"Agent Steve Nance." The agent reached out and shook Nate's hand. "I'm investigating a case that led me to Echo Mountain Rentals. When I arrived to question the owner, I found the door open, the office ransacked, and no one inside. I guess your witness assumed I was the perp." He nodded toward the building where Cassie sat on the front steps, her chin resting on her upturned palms.

A rush of relief washed over Nate. She was okay; not hurt, just frightened.

"I'd like to be brought up to speed on your investigation," Nate said to the agent. "Perhaps our murder is related."

"Of course. I have a lead I'm following up on in twenty minutes. Can we meet for lunch?"

"Sure. Healthy Eats Restaurant, one o'clock?"

"Sounds good."

Nate went to Cassie, rehearsing his lecture in his head before he said the words. Then he remembered how she didn't like being bossed around. If he wanted to keep her safe, he needed her cooperation, not her defiance. He couldn't afford to push her away.

"Cassie?" he greeted.

She looked up, her cheeks red. His gut clenched.

"Hey, you okay?" He sat beside her.

She shook her head. "I'm ashamed."

"Ashamed? Why?"

"I obviously overreacted. I mean the guy is an FBI agent, but the door was open and I got this feeling, and Bree said never to ignore that feeling, and then the guy comes outside and he's got a gun."

He placed a gentle hand against her back. "Cassie, you did not overreact. Someone *did* break into the office. That's a crime. You did the right thing by calling 911."

"I guess."

"It's not a guess. You acted responsibly."

She frowned slightly, fiddling with her key chain.

"What is it?" he said.

"No one's ever said that to me before." She glanced at him. "I appreciate it."

His heart raced, but not from fear or adrenaline. He slipped his hand off her back. "You know what I'd appreciate?"

"What?"

"If you didn't go anywhere alone for a while, just in case Len Pragner has friends in town."

"You think he does?"

"It's possible."

"Did you interrogate him?"

"I tried."

"What did he say?"

Nate ripped his gaze from her hopeful blue eyes. "Nothing helpful," he said. "But he knows who you are, which is why I'm concerned for your safety."

As he scanned the parking lot for signs of trouble, a silver minivan pulled up beside his patrol car.

"It's Mr. Anderson," she said.

The owner of Echo Mountain Rentals got out of his vehicle and cast a worried glance at the chief.

Nate stood to greet the middle-aged man. "Someone broke into your office."

Mr. Anderson glanced at Cassie. "Are you okay?"

"She called it in," Nate answered for her.

"I'm fine," Cassie said. "I showed up after the fact. You're lucky you didn't come in right at nine this morning."

"My assistant and I had a few stops to make."

A small blue sedan pulled into the lot. Mr. Anderson's assistant, Carol Trotter, got out of the car. "What's going on?" she asked, rushing up to them.

"Someone broke into the office," Mr. Anderson said.

The sixtysomething woman glanced at the building with rounded eyes.

"It's okay, he's gone," Nate said to ease her fear.

"But why?" she said. "We don't keep cash or anything valuable in there."

"Do you think this is related to the dead woman at the Whispering Pines cabin?" Mr. Anderson said.

"We're not sure," Nate said. "I'd like you to go through the office and see if anything's missing. That might help us determine motivation for the break-in."

"I can help," Cassie offered.

"Okay, but let's all wear gloves so as not to interfere with forensics."

Nate retrieved four pair of gloves from the patrol car.

When they went into the office, he noticed Cassie's rattled expression. Then she lifted her chin as if to say, *this isn't going to bother me.*

That's what he admired about her: her ability to act strong when she was feeling anything but powerful.

Cassie bent to pick up papers scattered on the floor. "Where would you like me to put these?"

"Stack them on the table," Mr. Anderson said. "We'll go through them."

"How about your files, Mr. Anderson?" Nate asked. "Does anything look off?"

"Carol is my file pro."

Carol analyzed the files strewn haphazardly on the floor. "It doesn't look like anything's missing."

They continued to go through the mess for a few minutes.

"This isn't good," Cassie said.

"What?" Nate questioned.

She held up an empty file folder, then another. "My personnel file is empty. So is Becca's."

"It probably just fell out somewhere." Carol got down on the floor and sifted through paperwork.

"What did you keep in those files?" Nate asked Mr. Anderson.

"Job applications, work reviews, property assignments."

"Our addresses and Social Security numbers were on those applications." Cassie glanced at Nate.

"Which address was on your application?" he asked.

"The farmhouse."

"That could be a good thing." Nate turned to Mr. Anderson. "Didn't you keep that type of sensitive information secured?"

"I lock it every night," Carol answered for her boss. "They must have picked the lock. What on earth would they want with personnel information?"

"I've got to warn Becca," Cassie said and raced out of the office.

* * *

Cassie paced outside, pressing her cell phone to her ear. "Come on, come on," she said under her breath. Why wasn't Becca answering? Was she in trouble?

Her voice mail picked up. "Hi, this is Becca. I can't take your call right now, so please leave a message."

"Becca, it's Cassie. Be careful. Someone stole our personnel files from the office so they know where you live, and we need to talk because I don't know what's going on and we could be in danger, or at least we were in danger until they arrested that guy last night, but still we don't know if he has a partner—"

A solid hand rested on her shoulder. She glanced into Nate's green eyes. "Take a breath," he offered. "Tell her to meet us at the police station."

Cassie nodded. "Becca, come to the police station. Chief Walsh and I will explain everything." She ended the call and nibbled at her lower lip.

"Come back inside." With a hand cupping her elbow, Nate led her into the office. "Was Becca working for you this morning?" Nate asked Mr. Anderson.

"No, she's off until Wednesday."

"She has a second job with Blackburn Adventures guiding tourists into the mountains," Cassie said. "Maybe she took a group out today."

"I'll check into it," Nate said. "In the meantime, other than personnel files, does anything else seem to be missing?" Nate directed his question to Mr. Anderson, who glanced at his assistant.

"Not that I can tell," Carol said. "I'll keep looking."

"Thanks. When forensics arrives, you and Mr. Anderson should clear out. Do you have another location where you can conduct business?"

"We can work out of one of the empty cabins," Mr. Anderson said.

"I'll have a patrol car stay here until you're finished. Also, Cassie needs a few days off until we sort this out."

"Nate—"

"Cassie, don't argue with me on this," he said.

"We completely understand. We're pretty slow for the next few weeks, so no worries," Mr. Anderson said.

"Thanks." Cassie handed him the manila envelope. "Sorry my paperwork is late."

"Totally understandable," Mr. Anderson said. "I'm glad you're okay."

Nate escorted Cassie outside to her car.

"You didn't have to apologize for late paperwork, either," he said.

"I don't want to lose this job."

"He seems like an understanding boss."

She narrowed her eyes at him. "Why do I get the feeling you've only said sorry, what, twice in your entire life?" she teased.

"Maybe three times," he countered.

She was surprised he'd joked back. "Wow, a whole three times."

"Hey, you don't have to point out my faults. I know them intimately."

Pointing out his shortcomings was not what she'd meant to do. "I wasn't trying to—"

"So, you'll head back to the resort now?" he interrupted.

"I'd like to help you find Becca."

"Cassie, this is a police investigation."

"At least let me call Blackburn Adventures. I have the number in my phone."

"Okay, go ahead."

Cassie called Blackburn, a family-owned company founded more than thirty years ago with an excellent reputation.

"Thank you for calling Blackburn Adventures. Sorry we missed your call. Please leave your name—"

Cassie glanced at Nate. "No one's answering. I don't like this. I'll run by her place to see if she's okay."

"Cassie—"

"What if she's in trouble?"

"I need to know you're safe at all times. That means going back to the resort. I'll swing by Becca's apartment."

"Okay, Chief." She got behind the wheel of her car and turned the key, but it wouldn't start. She tried again. Nothing.

She opened the door. "What else could possibly go wrong today?"

"Could be your battery," he said.

After a few minutes of trying to jump her battery with no success, Nate suggested it might be her alternator, or possibly something more serious.

"Come on," he said. "I guess you're with me."

With him? She liked the sound of that. Cassie walked a little too excitedly beside him but couldn't help herself. He motioned to a police officer.

"Officer Hough, keep an eye on Mr. Anderson and his assistant until they leave the premises. Get keys so you can give forensics access to the office."

"Yes, sir."

"Chief?" Carol said, coming toward them. "The only missing personnel files are Cassie and Becca's." She nodded at Cassie's car. "Is there a problem?"

"It won't start," Cassie offered.

"We'll be here for an hour or so if you want to leave the keys with me and call for a tow."

"That would be great." Cassie started to hand Carol her keys and hesitated. The key chain was her touchstone to the future and her glorious travel plans. She removed the car keys and handed them to Carol. "I appreciate it."

"Of course." Carol went back into the office.

Cassie made the call to have Ruby towed, and Nate led

her to the squad car. "I'll drop you at the resort and I'll go check on your friend."

"Nate, please take me with you. I'm worried about her. I've even got a key to her apartment for when I feed the cat if she's out of town." Cassie jangled her keys.

"I noticed you wouldn't part with the key chain. Those charms mean a lot to you, don't they?"

"Oh yeah. The cross and flower charms represent God and nature, and these three remind me I'm going to England, Australia, and France," she said, pointing to the respective charms. "Although I keep thinking I should add a charm for Switzerland, but haven't figured out what that is yet."

Realizing she was chattering away again, she stopped and glanced at Nate. A half smile curled his lips.

"Hang on, were you trying to change the subject? You were, weren't you?" she said. "Nate, come on, we need to check on Becca, and the resort is half an hour in the opposite direction of her apartment. That's a whole hour lost. Let me go with you."

Nate shook his head in surrender and opened the car door. "Okay, on one condition."

"What?" She shifted onto the front seat and buckled up.

"Follow my orders. I know you don't like to be told what to do, but I can't worry about you *and* do my job effectively, understand?"

"Of course."

He shut the door. He was worried about her? Could it be more than just an officer of the law worrying about a witness? It felt like more, but then Cassie didn't have a lot of experience reading between the lines when it came to men.

When he got behind the wheel of the car, he reached for the radio to call in. "Base, this is Chief Walsh. I'm heading to Becca Edwards's apartment at…" He glanced at Cassie.

"543 Wilshire."

"543 Wilshire," he said into the radio.

"Copy that, Chief."

He pulled out of the lot and headed toward town.

"Thanks," she said.

He shot her a quick glance, then refocused on the road. "For what?"

"Listening to me again."

"What... I don't understand."

"You respected my need to make sure my friend is okay."

"I respect a lot of things about you, Cassie."

"That's a first," she muttered.

"Meaning what?"

"It'll sound dumb."

"Try me."

"I don't feel like I get a lot of respect from my family."

"You mean Aiden?"

"And my mom, and Bree. Then again, Bree isn't too bossy, but my cousin Madeline..." She shook her head.

"What about her?"

"Never mind." Cassie glanced out the window, wondering why on earth she was exposing herself like this to Nate, of all people.

"I'd like to understand why you're thanking me, so maybe I can do it again," he said.

She snapped her gaze left and noticed a hint of a smile playing at the corner of his lips.

Frustration eased from her chest. She liked it when he smiled. She could almost feel it herself.

"Your cousin?" he prompted.

"Sometimes she makes me feel, I don't know, small. She's patronizing, and she teases me, and not always in a good way."

"Have you talked to her about it?"

"No."

"Don't you think you should?"

"I wouldn't know what to say," she admitted.

"Finding the right words is the toughest part."

"Did you ever have an uncomfortable talk with someone you cared about?"

"I did."

"What happened?"

"I lost her for a little while, but eventually it strengthened our relationship."

"Oh." So there *was* a woman in Nate's life. Cassie puzzled over that one, since he lived alone and never seemed to be with a woman during his off-hours.

"My sister," he clarified.

"Catherine? But she's so lovely and caring and patient—"

"Too patient. Do you know why she moved to Echo Mountain?"

"To open a restaurant?"

"To distance herself from Dylan's father, an abusive jerk."

"I had no idea."

"It's not something she's proud of, and the guy was sneaky about it. He'd scream in her face one night, act like nothing had happened the next morning and then bring her flowers after work. She never told me about it—Dylan did. It was about the time Dylan wanted to defend his mom that I got involved. I went to college with Chief Washburn's nephew, and we'd come to Echo Mountain to visit family on break. I thought it would be the perfect place for Catherine to get a fresh start."

"And she stopped talking to you because…?"

"She resented me telling her what to do, not that you can relate to that." He smiled.

Cassie smiled back and felt herself blush.

"Anyway, she fought me on the move until one day her ex chased Dylan around the house swinging a wooden chair. That was it. She called me and I made arrangements for her to move here. She got a job at a local restaurant, and a few years later the owner sold it to her. Shortly after that I—" he hesitated "—I had a career shift and Chief Washburn offered me a job. I was glad to move near my family. Catherine's got a wonderful life in Echo Mountain."

"But why was she upset with you for trying to help her?"

"Months after they'd moved here, she admitted she was ashamed that her little brother had saved her, and she said a part of her felt her husband's violent behavior was her fault."

"Nate, no, that's nonsensical."

"Human emotions. They don't always make sense. Like a mother who's overly protective of her grown daughter because she was sick as a child."

"But I'm not sick anymore."

"Emotions don't have to make sense to be real, Cassie. Your mom's worry is real."

"I know." She hesitated. "But it drives me nuts."

"Then tell her."

Cassie shook her head. "I could never hurt her feelings like that."

"And you won't hurt her when you take off on one of your trips because you're trying to get away from her?"

That gave her pause. "I never thought about it like that. What would I say to her?"

"You've got a solid relationship with God. Why don't you pray on it?"

Nate could hardly believe the words that had come out of his mouth. *Pray on it?*

Sure, why not? It made sense for a woman like Cassie to pray, a woman who needed to find her voice with her family or risk losing them forever.

And family was everything. Catherine and Dylan were Nate's family, along with the former chief, Aiden McBride, and a few search-and-rescue friends. Truth was, Nate's family had grown exponentially since his move to Echo Mountain.

After losing his partner, Nate would never take family for granted again.

A few minutes later, they pulled up to Becca's place.

Nate eyed the building for signs of trouble, yet all seemed quiet in the neighborhood.

Cassie placed a gentle hand on his arm. "Thanks."

The warmth from her hand drifted up and settled across his shoulders. "For what?"

"Helping me get perspective about my mom."

"That's the second time today you've thanked me. I'm getting pretty good at this." He shot her a smile and reached out. "Keys?"

She dropped them into his palm.

"You stay put, got it?" he said.

"Sure."

But halfway to the apartment building, a nagging sensation told him not to leave her behind.

He turned back and motioned for Cassie to join him. As she opened the door, her blue eyes widened with curiosity. "What's wrong?"

"Nothing. Just want to keep you close."

A contented smiled eased across her adorable face.

"In order to keep you safe," he clarified.

Her smile faded. "Of course."

He refocused on the apartment. Why did he have to say that?

Because he was being professional.

Because he wanted to keep the line firmly drawn between them.

Because you're a jerk.

They approached the building in silence, Cassie a few inches behind him to the right. The key gave them access to the front door, so they let themselves in and took the stairs to the second floor.

"Her apartment is around the corner," Cassie said.

"I'm sorry," he said, wanting to apologize for his rude nature.

"For what?" She led him down the hall and froze.

Becca's apartment door was cracked open.

"Nate," she whispered.

He grabbed her arm and pulled her behind him. He withdrew his firearm.

Here he thought keeping her close was the safe thing to do. He had no idea what he was walking into, but couldn't send her back to the squad car alone.

Focus, Nate. Focus.

Senses on high alert, he moved slowly toward Becca's door, Cassie right behind him, her hand against his back.

A crash echoed down the hall from inside the apartment.

He had no intention of leading Cassie into a dangerous situation. Pointing to the stairs, he leaned close, his lips practically touching her hair.

"Go upstairs and stay out of sight," he whispered.

She nodded and brushed soft fingertips against his cheek as if to say "be careful." The warmth gave him an added confidence he couldn't explain.

Still focused on the partially open door, he waited a good ten seconds until he knew Cassie was safely hidden. He shot a quick glance over his shoulder. Couldn't see her.

With the toe of his boot, he eased the door open and stepped inside.

EIGHT

Cassie clasped her hands together and prayed. She prayed that Becca was okay, and she prayed for Nate's safety.

She wasn't sure why she'd touched his cheek the way she had. It was instinctive. She needed to make that connection before he stormed into whatever was waiting for him in Becca's apartment.

Squeezing her hands tight, she prayed: *Dear Lord, please keep my friends safe in Your loving embrace. Let Your light shine upon us, Your love flow through us, and Your glory protect us.*

She realized, and not for the first time, that her stomach twisted into a pretzel-like knot at the thought of Nate being hurt, or worse.

Please God, keep him safe.

Because she wasn't sure how she would manage if anything happened to him. The image of his disoriented expression last night in his truck flashed through her mind. The look in his eyes, that faraway, confused look, stuck deep in her core. Nate was a tenacious, capable man who'd been broken trying to protect her.

"Cassie?"

Her eyes popped open, and she spied around the corner to the floor below. Nate motioned to her. "It's clear."

She released the breath she didn't know she'd been holding. It must have sounded like she gasped for air, because Nate was suddenly beside her.

"You okay?"

She nodded. "Who knew praying could be so exhausting?"

He pulled her against his chest in a brief hug as if to convince her she was safe. Which was exactly how she felt whenever he held her in his arms. The hug didn't last nearly long enough.

Not letting go of her hand, he led her to the second floor and into Becca's apartment.

"I think the cat knocked something over," he said. "Saw him run into the bedroom."

"Probably hiding under the bed. You should shut the door to keep him safe."

Nate released her. "Don't touch anything. It's a crime scene."

"Is Becca…?"

"Not here," he said as he closed the bedroom door.

She sighed with relief.

"Detective Vaughn is on the way. Could you try Blackburn Adventures again to see if they have any information about Becca?"

"Sure." Cassie made the call, her eyes scanning the disheveled living room: books strewn about, cushions ripped off the sofa and pillows shredded into pieces. The thought of a man slitting innocuous pillows with a large blade made her cringe. She clung to the hope that Becca wasn't home when the intruder destroyed her apartment.

"You've reached Blackburn Adventures—"

Cassie ended the call. "It's voice mail again."

Footsteps pounded up to the second floor. Detective Vaughn rushed into the apartment. "Any sign of Becca Edwards?"

"No," Nate said. "We've been trying to reach her employer, but they're not answering. Found the premises tossed. I'll leave you in charge here while I head over to Blackburn Adventures to see if Becca showed up for work."

"And there's a cat in the bedroom," Cassie offered.

Nate motioned Cassie toward the door, but hesitated and turned to Agent Vaughn. "I'm meeting with FBI agent Nance at one o'clock."

Vaughn snapped her attention to him. "What have the Feds got to do with this?"

"He's working a case that led him to Echo Mountain Rentals."

"Led him how?" She narrowed her eyes.

"I'll find out at lunch and I'll let you know."

"Thanks, Chief."

Cassie felt like she was missing something; there was subtext to that exchange. The way Detective Vaughn reacted to the mention of FBI involvement ignited a spark of tension.

Once they got downstairs, Cassie asked, "Is she...upset?"

Nate glanced at her as he opened the door and led her outside.

"About the FBI?" Cassie prompted.

"Nah, it's a territorial thing. Sometimes various law enforcement agencies don't play well together in the sandbox. She's probably worried the agent won't share information."

They got into the squad car and pulled away.

"Sharing information is crucial, it's—" he hesitated "—well, it can affect a man's life."

"Yeah, I'm worried about Becca's life right now."

"Hey, don't go there. These guys usually don't like breaking in when someone's home. It complicates things. The assailant probably waited until she left for work this morning."

Cassie glanced out the window, wondering how yesterday at this time life seemed so simple, so easy: work to make money so she could travel. No complications, no second thoughts.

"Cassie?"

His deep voice speaking her name set off a round of second, third and fourth thoughts about her leaving Echo Mountain.

She glanced at him, steeling herself against his concerned expression.

"I'll do everything within my power to find and help your friend," he said.

"I know, thank you. That gives me great peace."

"I wouldn't go that far," he muttered, eyeing the road.

"Why not?"

He shook his head as if the conversation was over, but she wasn't giving up. She'd openly shared her frustrations about family and the challenges of battling her childhood medical condition. It would help her understand this guarded man if she knew a little about his past.

"You said you used to come here with Chief Washburn's nephew on break?" she started.

"Yes."

"So you went to college?"

"I did."

"And studied what, criminology?"

"Actually, got a degree in psychology. Was going to do law school, but decided to join the Chicago PD instead."

"What was that like compared to being a police officer here?"

He shot her a wry smile. "Different."

"I'll bet. Why did you leave? To be near Catherine?"

"Mostly."

Cassie waited. She sensed he wanted to talk, but rarely opened up. To anyone. Who would he confess his past to, anyway? As the local police chief, he had to maintain a strong, professional demeanor. Revealing any flaws or imperfections could make people feel insecure.

How unfair, Cassie thought. People were human, not perfect. But it was also human nature to want to look up to people in leadership positions, sometimes even put them on pedestals.

"I don't mean to be nosy," she said.

"Oh yes, you do." He shot her a quick glance and winked. "Just promise me none of this will end up in the community blog."

"Nate, do you honestly think I'd—"

"I'm kidding."

"Because I want you to trust me as much as I trust you, and with everything I've told you over the past twenty-four hours, you're one of the most trusted people in my life right now."

"I'm honored."

Redirecting her attention out the window, Cassie felt offended by his quip about her publishing his life story in the community blog. She thought he knew her better than that, knew that she wouldn't ever share a confidence. Then again, how could he know that? It wasn't like they were good friends, or something more serious like boyfriend and girlfriend. He was the police chief doing his job, and she'd been randomly targeted for some reason.

The constant threat of danger must be wearing on her, that's all. It was silly to be offended because Nate wanted to keep his secrets to himself.

"My partner was killed."

She snapped her gaze to study his profile. He would not look at her.

"Along with a witness he was guarding," he added.

"Oh, Nate, I am so sorry."

"I feel responsible."

"What? Why?"

Again, he shook his head, as if to indicate that was as much as he could share.

She waited, interlacing her fingers to remind herself that God was present and listening, and could hopefully ease the burden she knew was weighing on Nate's heart.

They reached a stoplight and he glanced at her. "He didn't trust me with the truth."

"Which was?"

"He and the female witness—" He hesitated and redirected his attention to the light. It turned green and he pulled into the intersection. "They'd grown close."

"And that isn't allowed, right?"

"It's ill advised. If you're distracted by a pretty face you can't do your job."

She wondered if they were still talking about his partner, or if the comment was meant for her as another warning. Like he hadn't given her enough warnings, drawing a firm line between them over and over again. Suddenly it hit her why it was so important for him to maintain his distance.

"I don't understand why your partner's death is your fault," she said.

"Maybe I could have prevented it if I'd known what was going on. I would have at least been there as backup, knowing he couldn't be in love with the witness and effectively protect her."

"You can't blame yourself for his choices."

"Yeah, well…" A few seconds passed. "I was devastated by his death. When I pressed one of the guys, he said Dean didn't tell me about the affair because he knew I'd judge him. It was just like my sister taking that garbage from her ex for years and not telling me. Why are people afraid to tell me things? Am I that intimidating or scary or what?"

Cassie actually welcomed Nate's uncharacteristic rant. When she'd share her frustrations with God, it often eased the pressure in her heart.

"By your silence, I guess that means yes," he said.

"Actually, I was waiting to see if you were done." She motioned with her hands. "Come on, there's gotta be more in there."

"You're teasing me."

"I most certainly am not. I'm impressed by your honesty, and now don't freak out, but also your vulnerability."

"That's not what a man likes to hear, Cassie, especially one who's supposed to be protecting you."

"It means you're human. You feel things just like the rest of us."

He frowned. "That's how the town sees me? As some kind of unfeeling robot?"

She touched his arm. "No, but sometimes the whole strong, silent type thing makes people uncomfortable. When someone's unusually reserved, like you, people wonder what you're thinking, and because they don't know what's going on up here—" she touched the side of his head "—they make things up. Stuff like 'he thinks I'm an idiot' or 'he doesn't like my choices.' It's just human nature."

"So what, I'm supposed to talk all the time like—" He stopped abruptly.

"Like me?" Cassie finished for him. "It's okay, I know I'm a chatterbox. But no, you don't have to jibber-jabber to ease the tension with other people. Just be a little more open, you know, softer, like your friend Will Rankin."

"Will's got two little girls to soften his edges."

"Well, you have friends, lots of friends, to help you practice your communication skills."

"Maybe if I'd had better skills my partner would have confided in me."

"And you would have said what?"

"I would have told him it was a bad idea, that getting romantically involved on the job was insanity."

"Which would have felt like he was being judged."

"Being brutally honest is the only way I know how to communicate. I was hoping a little of that would rub off on you."

"What is that supposed to mean?"

"You could be more honest with your family."

"I can't risk hurting their feelings. I told you that."

"Look at us, I'm brutally honest and you're brutally careful not to hurt anyone's feelings."

"It creates a kind of strange balance, doesn't it?" she said, not censoring her words before they left her mouth. She wondered if she'd scared him back into his cave.

"Yeah, it sort of creates balance," he said in a soft voice.

"Do you have anything else to get off your chest?" she said in a teasing tone.

"Actually, I'm good for now."

"Then will you do me a favor?"

"What's that?"

"Stop blaming yourself for your partner's death."

"I'll try."

"I've got an idea, how about surrendering the guilt to God? Does that sound doable?"

"I've never… I don't really have a connection to God."

"That's okay. He has a connection to you. Open your heart to the idea?"

"I guess I can do that."

Nate wasn't sure why he'd agreed to opening up to God, but for the first time in his life the idea didn't seem all that foreign. It was probably Cassie's nurturing personality and hopeful attitude that got through to that empty spot in his heart where he knew others found their faith.

He'd envied his friend Will, a man of faith who always seemed so grounded, even as he balanced being a single parent with work and volunteering for SAR. But Nate figured the window of opportunity had passed, that he'd ignored God for too long and he'd missed his chance.

Cassie thought differently.

She continually amazed him by the way she talked, listened and counseled. Which was great, except that she was a witness in danger and this was a repeat of his partner's situation. If Nate would have gotten in Curt's face about falling in love with a witness, Nate deserved to give himself that same lecture.

Falling in love? Was that what was happening between him and Cassie?

No, Nate wasn't thinking clearly due to lack of sleep. He knew the reality of the situation, and his focus had to be about protecting her. After they arrested the perpetrator or perpetrators and closed the investigation, *that* would be the time to see if there could be something more between Nate and Cassie.

Only one problem: it was her life's dream to travel, and he'd be a jerk to do anything to get in her way, like asking her out on a date.

"You think she's in trouble, don't you?" Cassie said.

Nate snapped his attention to her. "I'm sorry?"

"You get this look when you're worried about something. You think Becca's in serious trouble?"

"No, I was thinking about something else."

I was thinking about you.

"Care to share?" she said.

"Not at present, no." Could he ever speak his truth to Cassie?

Cassie's phone rang. "It's Blackburn Adventures," she said, eyeing the screen.

"Could you put it on speaker?"

She pressed the speaker button. "Hello?"

"This is Blackburn Adventures. I saw multiple calls from this number. Can I help you with something?"

"This is Echo Mountain Police Chief Walsh. With whom am I speaking?"

"Wendy Longmire, trail guide."

"May I speak with whoever is in charge, please?" Nate asked.

"Sure, I'll get my boss."

Cassie nibbled her lower lip. Nate shot her what he hoped was a reassuring nod, but even he didn't know where this would lead.

"This is Jeff Porter, can I help you?"

"Police Chief Walsh here. I'm looking for Becca Edwards."

"She's leading a group up the west side of Echo Mountain. They left at six this morning."

"I need to contact her. Is that possible?"

"Let's see…by now they'll be a few miles west of Rattlesnake Pass. I can try, but reception tends to be hit or miss on that side of the mountain."

"I'll be there in about five minutes. In the meantime, can you tell me how she seemed this morning when she came to work?"

"Hang on. Hey, Wendy, how was Becca this morning?"

"She seemed okay," Wendy said from the background. "Excited about some trip she and her boyfriend were planning. I think they were leaving after today's hike."

"Did she seem anxious or worried?" Nate asked.

"No, sir."

"Thanks."

"Do you want me to try to contact her before you get here?" Jeff said.

"No, I'd rather you wait."

"Will do."

"See you soon." He nodded at Cassie, who ended the call. His fingers tightened around the steering wheel. None of this made sense.

"What?" she said.

He shot her a quick glance.

"You're gripping the steering wheel so tight your knuckles are turning white."

"I can't seem to make sense of this. Someone's after Becca, and she's planning to leave town, but she takes a group up into the mountains? If she's fleeing the jurisdiction she must know she's a target, right? But then why go to work and act like everything's fine?"

"You almost make it sound like she's a suspect."

"Right now she's acting like one."

A few minutes later they pulled into the Blackburn Adventures lot. Jeff, the manager, introduced himself.

"I'm Chief Walsh and this is Cassie McBride."

"Right, Aiden's little sister," Jeff said.

"That's me."

He led them into the office and clicked on a high-powered radio.

"Becca, this is base, over," Jeff said. "Becca, come in, over." A few seconds passed.

"Why isn't she answering?" Cassie said.

"Like I said, bad reception," Jeff explained. "If they're in trouble someone will hit the locator beacon."

"How many people did she take up there?" Nate asked with concern. Not only was Becca in danger, but potentially her entire group.

Jeff eyed a clipboard. "Looks like seven."

"Could you give her another try?" Nate pressed.

"Becca, this is base. We need you to check in, over."

Scratchy silence echoed across the line.

"When do you expect them back?" Nate asked.

"About one o'clock."

Nate had agreed to meet the FBI agent at that time, but needed to be here when Becca returned.

"Hello? Hello, are you there?" a voice said through the radio.

"Becca, is that you, over?" Jeff responded.

"No…she's gone!" a female voice said.

NINE

Cassie's heart leaped into her throat.

"Gone, what do you mean, gone?" Jeff said. "Who is this?"

"Tanya Holmes. I've got a little hiking experience so they put me in charge."

Jeff clicked the radio so Tanya couldn't hear them. "This is a novice group," he said to Nate. "Little or no hiking experience to speak of."

"Let me." Nate took the radio.

"Tanya, this is Police Chief Walsh. When did Becca go missing?"

"About an hour ago. We stopped to eat lunch. She said she was going to check the trail up ahead because of bear sightings. She never came back."

"Is everyone okay?"

"For the most part, but one of the gals twisted her ankle when we tried to find Becca."

"The hiker who injured her ankle, is she mobile?"

"We were just trying to figure that out."

"Please assess the situation and let me know."

"Okay, hang on."

Cassie studied Nate's profile and marveled at his calm and confident demeanor in the midst of a crisis. Somehow his controlled reaction took the edge off the panic swirling in Cassie's stomach.

"Chief?" Tanya said through the radio.

"Yes, Tanya."

"Carly is unable to put pressure on her ankle."

"I'll dispatch search and rescue. Do you know your exact coordinates?"

"We're at the Lake Mirage Overlook."

Jeff pinpointed it on the map.

"Tanya, it should take them about ninety minutes to get to you," Nate said.

"A few of the guys want to head back down," she said.

"I'd prefer everyone stay together."

"I'll tell them."

"Which direction was Becca headed when you last saw her?"

"North on Chinook Trail."

"Hang tight. Help will be there ASAP."

"Okay, thanks."

Nate clicked off the radio and pulled out his phone.

"Ninety minutes is pushing it," Jeff said.

"You're not familiar with SAR," Nate countered. "It becomes a contest to see who can get there first."

As Nate drove Cassie to a safe location so he could join the search, she considered what could have happened to her friend, a seasoned climber.

"I'll find her, Cassie," he said.

She glanced across the car at Nate, realizing he knew her so well he could sense what she was thinking.

"I want to go with you."

"Not an option. You know that." He pulled onto Resort Drive and only then did she realize where he was taking her.

"Nate—"

"Echo Mountain Resort has the best security in the county. I know you don't like being told what to do, but this once, could you be okay with my plan to keep you safe?"

Her automatic reaction was to argue, to come up with all sorts of reasons why she didn't want to be dumped at the resort into the midst of her overbearing family, but she stopped herself. There was something about his voice, a hint of desperation that made her reconsider.

"What's the plan?" she said.

"You'll stay at Echo Mountain Resort while I'm gone, either in your sister's cottage or in a resort room, but please don't go anywhere alone." He paused. "I'm sorry if that sounds like an order, but I don't know a nicer way to say it."

"I understand."

And she did. Somehow she was able to appreciate Nate's concern for her well-being without growing defensive.

"What's wrong?" he said.

"Why do you think something's wrong?"

"You're being too agreeable. I mean it, Cassie, no leaving the resort."

"I know."

"And stay out of sight if possible."

"Ten-four, Chief."

He pulled up to the front of the resort, got out of the car and opened the door for her, his eyes scanning the parking lot.

"I got it from here," Aiden said, approaching them.

"I thought you'd be on the team heading up to Lake Mirage Overlook," Nate said.

"Too much going on here today. Besides, I heard it was just a sprained ankle."

"And Becca's missing," Cassie said.

"Missing?" Aiden questioned, looking at Nate.

"I'll know more when I get up there."

Aiden nodded at Cassie. "Okay, I'll take care of trouble here."

Cassie would have normally shot off a retort to her brother, but she couldn't be bothered. Not when she feared for Nate's safety. Who knew what trouble he'd find once he reached the spot where Becca had disappeared?

"Be careful," she said, only this time she didn't touch his cheek. She wrapped her arms around his waist and gave him a hug. When he didn't return the gesture she thought maybe she'd crossed a line. But it was her way of wishing him well.

Just as she released him, his arms tightened around her back and he held on for a few seconds. He leaned forward and whispered, "Be safe. Promise?"

"Promise," she uttered, barely able to speak against the ball of emotion tightening in her throat.

He released her and without making eye contact, got into his car and drove off.

It was almost as if the hug had energized him, Nate thought as he practically sprinted up the incline of the trail. The first team radioed that they were nearly at the site, and Nate wanted to get there as quickly as possible. He'd called his sister at Healthy Eats, described the FBI agent, and asked her to let him know Nate wouldn't be back for their meeting.

Joining Nate on the mission was Officer "Red" Carrington and Nate's friend Will Rankin, a widower who was dating Detective Vaughn. None of the men spoke much as they motored up the mountain with purpose.

The other team would probably take the lead on assisting the injured hiker, while Nate and Red would search the surrounding area for clues as to what happened to Becca. He'd send Will back down with the first team, not wanting to put the single father in danger.

"Hey, speedy," Will said, short of breath.

Nate glanced at his friend.

"I'm in good shape and you're killin' me here. Trevor's team is perfectly capable of dealing with a sprained ankle."

It wasn't just the thought of the injured hiker that made Nate run uphill. It was the look on Cassie's face, the look of worry about her friend being in trouble.

Nate would do anything to ease her fears, to make her smile.

"Nate, say something, grunt, anything," Will pushed.

Red chuckled.

Nate slowed down a bit. "Sorry."

"What's really going on here?" Will asked.

"Guess I'm worried about Becca Edwards. She's gone missing."

"I know that, but I assumed she slipped and took a tumble or something. Is there more to this?"

Nate motioned for Red to hike ahead, while Nate hung back with his friend. "Her apartment was tossed. We can't rule out foul play, which is why I want you to head down with team one once we get to the injured hiker."

"What are you going to do?"

"Red and I will search the area for clues, some indication as to what happened to her."

"Well, if she needed help, she should have activated her locator beacon."

"True. In a way, I'm hoping she intentionally disappeared."

"That makes no sense. A trail guide wouldn't abandon her tour group."

"There's a lot that hasn't made sense since we found a dead woman at the Whispering Pines cabin."

"Yeah, I heard about that."

Nate glanced at him. "News gets around in a small town."

"Smaller when you're dating the lead detective." Will smiled.

Nate hadn't seen him smile like that for years, since his wife had died.

For a brief second Nate wondered if that's how he looked when he thought about Cassie.

"Speaking of dating…" Will started. "You been out on any lately?"

"No time."

"You seem to be spending a lot of time with Cassie."

"She's a witness in a murder investigation."

"I meant before that."

"She comes into the station to get ideas for the community blog."

"She's a sweet lady."

"Who's traveling to the far corners of the world once she gets enough money."

"Maybe she just needs a good reason to stay."

"Can we focus on the mission?" Nate said.

Will winked. "Which one?"

"Chief, I see the group up ahead," Red called out.

Nate and Will picked up their pace and reached the tour group within minutes. The first team seemed to have it under control. They had wrapped the ankle, secured the hiker to the litter, and were ready to head down.

"Sorry if this was a wasted trip for you," Nate said to Will.

"Any day out here in the mountains is a blessing, not a waste. I'd be happy to stay and help you look for Becca."

Nate recalled the incident when Will suffered from amnesia after being injured by a criminal in the mountains. He would not put his friend at risk again.

"No, we're good." Nate looked at the hikers, who assembled to head back down. "May I have your attention?"

They glanced in his direction.

"I'm Chief Walsh with Echo Mountain PD. Who spoke with your trail guide before she disappeared?"

A woman raised her hand.

"Are you Tanya?" Nate asked.

"Yes, sir."

"I'll need to talk to you for a second. Anyone else speak with Becca Edwards?"

They shook their heads that they hadn't.

"I'm asking for a refund, that's for sure," a fiftyish man said.

"Don't be so heartless, Roger," a woman about the same age scolded. "What if something happened to the poor girl?"

Roger shrugged.

"So, no one else spoke with the guide, or noticed anything unusual?" Nate said.

"She seemed nervous," a man offered. He was in his midforties, wearing a blue ski cap with the letter *B* on the front, and dark sunglasses.

"And you are?"

"Owen Banks." He shook Nate's hand.

"How did she seem nervous, Owen?"

"The way she looked around, like she was worried about something."

"There are bears out here," Will offered.

Nate looked at Tanya. "Did you sense Becca was nervous?"

"Not particularly."

"Thanks." Nate motioned for them to rejoin the group.

"You sure you don't want me to help search for her?" Will offered.

"I'm sure."

Nate sent the hikers back down. He and Red got to work following the trail in the opposite direction, looking for clues.

About an hour later, Nate spotted a small glove on the ground. He picked it up. "Could be Becca's."

"Chief," Red pointed up ahead. A woman's hiking boot lay in the middle of the trail.

Twenty feet from the boot was a dark green jacket.

"What happened out here?" Red muttered.

"Let's pack this stuff up and keep moving."

A few hours later the sky grew dark and Nate sensed a storm brewing. Rather than backtrack, Nate decided to consider other options.

"Hang on a second." Nate pulled out his binoculars and the topographical map. He handed the map to Red. "Can you find us the quickest way down?"

Nate peered through the binoculars, scanning the immediate area for signs of Becca. Could she still be out here, held captive by someone? He didn't figure this for an animal attack because her jacket wasn't torn, nor were the other items of clothing they'd found: the other glove, a scarf and a knit hat.

"Huh," Red said.

"What?"

"If we veer left in about half a mile, the trail leads straight down to Echo Mountain Resort."

A chill raced down Nate's spine. Cassie was at the resort.

"Let's move."

* * *

It had been nearly five hours without word from Nate. Through a slit in the resort room curtains, Cassie watched the sky grow dark with angry clouds. She couldn't stop thinking about Nate, worrying about him. To distract herself, she'd turn the television on and then turn it off, irritated by the inane programs that seemed to be on every channel. She wanted him to call or text or something.

A soft knock echoed across the room. She rushed to the door, hoping...

Instead of seeing Nate through the peephole, she saw Bree with Dasher in one arm and a grocery bag in the other.

Cassie swung open the door. "Hey."

"Brought you dinner," Bree said, waltzing into the room. "Ham and cheese melt sandwiches, fruit salad and raspberry brownies." She turned and narrowed her eyes, studying Cassie. "No? I thought you liked raspberry brownies."

"I do, it's not that."

"What then?" She put Dasher down and the dog sniffed his way around the room. "Wait, did Mom say something to make you feel guilty about not staying with her? I know she was upset when you said you wanted your own room. I guess I was a little miffed you didn't want to stay with me either, but—"

"I haven't heard from Nate."

"Where is he?"

"He went to search for Becca. She disappeared while leading a tour group up Echo Mountain," Cassie said, her voice pitching.

"Oh honey, I'm sorry." Bree gave Cassie a hug and patted her back. "I'm sure he'll find her." She broke the hug and looked into Cassie's eyes. "Becca's a resourceful woman. If she's in trouble, she'll figure out a way to signal the chief."

"I hope you're right."

"C'mon, let's eat something. Chocolate always makes you feel better."

* * *

Within the hour Cassie had managed to consume a sandwich and two brownies. "I was hungrier than I thought. Thanks for bringing all this food by."

"Sure. Guess you're lonely without your bodyguard." Bree smiled.

"Don't start."

"You guys do make a cute couple."

"How is that possible? He's intense and brooding, and I'm chatterbox Sally."

"It's perfect. He never has to talk and you don't have to compete for attention like you always had to do with us growing up."

Cassie picked up Dasher and held him in her lap. "Don't get me wrong, Nate's a nice guy, but we want completely different things out of life."

"Like?" Bree leaned back and nibbled a brownie.

"He's got a good job in town as chief, versus me wanting to travel."

"Police chiefs get vacation."

"Not for months at a time." She shook her head. "What am I talking about? We've never even been on a date."

"Maybe because you haven't been quiet long enough for him to ask?" She winked.

"Or he's not interested."

"Trust me." Bree started packing up the plates. "He's interested. Are you?"

Cassie considered the burn in her stomach. She'd just eaten, so it wasn't hunger. She was deeply worried about Nate. On some level she knew she liked him a lot more than as a friend.

"You're taking a long time to answer," Bree said.

"I can't be interested. It makes no logical sense."

Bree chuckled. "And when did you become Miss Pragmatic? Love isn't logical, little sister. Look at me and Scott. There is no way I should have fallen in love with a wounded stranger in the mountains. But I did." Bree reached out and touched Cassie's arm. "Love is surprising and wonderful and glorious. You need to trust it." She stood. "I'm going to the lobby to get a cup of tea. You want one?"

"Sure."

Bree went to the door. "Do you have a preference?"

"Anything will be fine," Cassie said, gently stroking the dog's fur.

"Hey, Cassie?"

Cassie glanced at her sister.

"I'm sure Nate will call soon."

Just then the nightstand phone rang.

"See," Bree said with a smile and shut the door.

Still holding Dasher, Cassie went to answer the phone, wondering why Nate hadn't called her cell.

"Hello?" she answered.

"Your friend is dead," a deep male voice said. "You're next, unless you—"

Cassie slammed down the phone and stepped back. It rang again. And kept ringing. What should she do? Nate ordered her not to go anywhere alone, so she shouldn't leave the room. But now a threatening man was calling. Did he know her room number? No, the front desk wouldn't give out that information.

She couldn't stand the ringing phone, so she unplugged it from the wall. She was safe. No one could get to her in this room.

Her cell rang and she hesitated before answering. Now she was being paranoid. She pulled it out of her pocket and eyed the screen. It was Nate. Relief washed over her.

"Nate, they keep calling so I unplugged—"

Pounding on the sliding glass door made her shriek.

TEN

The dog burst into a round of high-pitched barks.

"Cassie, what's wrong?" Nate said.

"The slider, someone's trying to get in."

"Cassie, it's Tony!" a muffled voice called from the other side of the glass. "Open the door! I need to talk to you!"

"Cassie!" Nate said through the line.

"It's Tony, Becca's boyfriend. Maybe he knows what happened to her."

Cassie whipped open the curtain. A wild-eyed Tony motioned to the door. Sliding it open, Cassie said, "What are you doing here?"

He eyed the phone. "Who are you talking to?"

"Chief Walsh, he's—"

Tony snatched the phone out of her hand and turned it off.

"Hey, I was talking."

"Listen to—"

"You owe me an explanation. Becca disappeared from her tour group and they sent out a search team and—"

"Enough!" he said.

Cassie bit her tongue, wanting to give him a piece of her mind for raising his voice. Instead, Dasher protested for her, barking his displeasure.

"Shut that thing up," Tony said. "I've gotta talk to you."

"Don't speak to us that way."

He reached for the dog, but Cassie turned away in a protective posture. "I'll put him in the bathroom." She marched across the room and kissed the dog on the head. "Just for a few minutes, Dasher."

She shut the door and turned to Tony. "Give me my phone."

"After we talk." He slipped her phone into his pocket.

Trusting her instincts, Cassie kept her position a good ten

feet away from Tony. His wild black hair practically stood straight up, and his skin was unusually pale, almost white, accentuating dark circles under his eyes.

"What happened to Becca?" she demanded.

"It's a long story."

"Give me the quick version."

He paced the small room. "It was supposed to be easy. No one would notice."

"Tony, I have no idea what you're talking about."

He stopped right in front of her. "You need to come with me."

"I don't think so."

"You have to, Cassie. Becca needs you."

"Why, is she hurt?"

"Just come, please?"

Three soft knocks echoed from the resort room door. "Hey, I've got tea, open up," Bree said.

"Yes, let us in," her mother added.

As Cassie started for the door, Tony grabbed her arm. "If you want to keep your family safe, you won't involve them in this."

"In what? Let me go." Cassie tried to wrench free.

Tony whipped out a gun. "I didn't want to use this, but you're not listening to me." His eyes flared with panic.

"If you're in trouble, Nate can help," she offered.

"No one can help, especially not the police."

"Cassie!" Bree pounded.

Tony flung out his arm and pointed the gun at the door. Panic flooded Cassie's chest.

"Don't you dare fire that thing."

"Then come with me."

Cassie grabbed her purple bag as Tony pulled her toward the sliding door. Bree's insistent pounding and the dog's echoed barking filled the room with chaos.

Going with him was her best choice. She didn't think Tony was a violent guy, but right now he seemed irrational beyond words. She wouldn't risk him discharging the weapon out of frustration and hurting her family.

Tony led her outside into the dark night, his fingers pinching her arm. He picked up his pace, half jogging toward a beat-up car. Cassie kept her head down and her eyes averted, not wanting to draw attention from innocent bystanders. She didn't know what Tony might do.

"Cassie!" Aiden shouted from the south entrance.

She was simultaneously relieved and terrified. Aiden would jump into a burning fire for someone he cared about, which meant he'd charge Tony and get a bullet in the gut for his trouble.

"I'm fine!" she shouted back. "Going to see a friend!"

"You're not supposed to leave!"

Tony rushed to his car and shoved her into the passenger side. "Move over. You're driving."

She did as ordered, glancing once in the rearview mirror. Both Aiden and the resort's security manager, Scott, Bree's boyfriend, were racing toward them.

"Go!" Tony shouted.

Her trembling hands put the car in Drive. Pressing down on the accelerator, she felt a tear warm her cheek.

I can't die yet. I haven't been to Australia or France.

I haven't been on a date with Nate Walsh.

Oh, what ridiculous thoughts flooded her brain when her life was being threatened.

"Faster!" he shouted.

She applied more pressure and they sped off. Her fear dissolved into anger. Once again, she was at the mercy of someone else's control, just like the disease that had dominated her childhood.

"If you're going to kill me you should at least tell me what's going on," she snapped.

He sighed, and it seemed like all the air was sucked out of him. "I'm not going to kill you," he said, and lowered the weapon.

"Then what's with the gun?"

"I need your help and I can't involve the police."

"Because you broke the law?"

"No…maybe… I don't know."

He sounded so defeated that she started to feel sorry for him, but caught herself.

"Don't you ever threaten my family again, you hear me?" she said.

"Yeah."

"I want my phone back."

He tossed it onto the dashboard.

"Is Becca okay?" she said, pocketing her phone.

"I don't know."

"You mean you're not taking me to see her?"

"No, sorry. I had to do something to get you to come with me."

Cassie raised an eyebrow at the gun in his lap. "Like that wasn't enough?"

"You're more stubborn than I thought. You have to help. I'm freaking out here."

"Tell me what happened."

"Becca was supposed to meet me at three this afternoon, but she didn't show up. No call, no text, nothing."

Cassie couldn't bring herself to tell him about the mystery phone call from a man claiming Becca was dead. It could send him into a downward spiral, and besides, the call might have been a manipulation to rattle Cassie's nerves.

"I went by her apartment and cop cars were everywhere," he continued.

"That's because someone broke in. They slashed cushions and tossed furniture. Do you know what they were looking for?"

He leaned back against the headrest. "Maybe."

"Clue me in."

"Money."

"Becca works two jobs to make rent. What money?"

He shook his head. "I can't."

"You'd better."

"I messed up, okay? There was so much of it and I didn't think they'd notice."

"Notice what?"

"Stop asking so many questions!"

"Hey, bub, you've taken me hostage so I'm allowed to ask as many questions as I like. Where are we going, by the way?"

"Somebody wants to meet you." He glanced at her, then away. "He'll help us get Becca back if you meet with him."

"Because he thinks I have something he wants? I don't have anything, Tony. You're dragging me into—"

"Just shut up!" he shouted.

Cassie pursed her lips, wanting to give him a lecture of a lifetime. Instead, she strategized ways to get help without being accidentally shot by Becca's crazy boyfriend.

"What's that?" Tony said, staring out the front windshield.

A car straddled the two-lane road up ahead, blocking traffic.

A patrol car.

"Go around it! Go around it!"

"But there's a drop off!"

Tony pressed his foot on top of hers, gunning the engine. To avoid a collision, she jerked the wheel right. They clipped the cruiser and slid off the road, barreling into the forest.

Heading straight for a tree.

"No!" she cried.

She jerked the wheel.

The car spun.

The back end slammed into a tree. The engine sputtered and died. She pinched her eyes shut, her heart pounding in her throat.

Breathe, she coached herself. *You're okay.*

"Cassie!"

Hearing Nate's voice made her feel better than okay.

She pried her eyes open and tried to focus on the man running toward her in the distance.

Then she remembered: Tony had a gun. She wanted to call out to Nate, to warn him, but struggled to get her voice back.

Backup was on the way. Nate couldn't wait. He sprinted toward the car Aiden had described as the kidnapper's.

Whoever had taken Cassie was in for a long night's interrogation. As he got closer, Nate could tell Cassie's eyes were open and she looked fairly coherent. He reached for his firearm, but was hesitant to use it. Opening fire on an assailant with Cassie in the middle was not an option.

"No!" she shouted at Nate just as…

A gunshot pierced the crisp night air.

Nate ducked, but not quick enough. A slow burn seared across his upper arm. Nothing, not even a gunshot wound, would stop him from getting to her. He'd have to be smart about it. Dropping to the ground, he crawled toward the car, clenching his teeth against the pain.

A young man in a black hoodie and jeans took off into the forest. Nate was about to pursue him when the perp turned and fired off multiple shots in Nate's direction.

With the car still between them.

Nate could only hope Cassie had the presence of mind to duck.

Staying low, Nate continued toward the car, assuming the perp's goal was to get away quickly and he couldn't do that with a hostage. Nate peered above the surrounding brush. The guy had disappeared into the forest. It made no sense for Nate to pursue him. The perp had the advantage of camouflage, and Nate would be an easy target.

He reached the car and cracked open the driver's side door. The old car didn't have an air bag. Nate searched Cassie's face for cuts and bruises.

"You okay?" he asked.

She glanced at his jacket and her eyes widened. "You've been shot." She started to unbuckle her seat belt.

"Don't move until the ambulance comes."

"I'm not hurt, but…" Her voice trailed off. She closed her eyes and took a deep breath, then another.

He suspected the full impact of what just happened—kidnapping and gunfire—must have finally hit her.

"Cassie?"

"I'm okay," she said. "Just scared."

He stroked her golden-blond hair. "There's nothing 'just' about being scared. Did the guy threaten you with a gun?"

She nodded. "It was Tony, Becca's boyfriend."

"Why did he take you hostage?"

"To meet someone who would help Tony find Becca, I think, I don't know for sure. But before that, at the resort, a man called my room. He had a deep, scratchy voice and said my friend was dead and I'd be next unless, but I hung up. Tony banged on the door. I let him in, I shouldn't have, because Bree and Mom wanted to come in and Tony pulled a gun and aimed it at the door and—"

"Shh, it's okay. Breathe." He continued to stroke her soft hair, hoping it would ease her anxiety.

She glanced at him. "I should be helping you. Let me out so I can put pressure on your wound."

"It's a flesh wound, no big deal. Relax until the EMTs check you out."

The wail of a siren echoed down the two-lane highway.

"What happened in the mountains?" she asked.

He hesitated, not wanting to upset her further.

"Nate, what is it?"

"We'll talk about it later." He took her hand. "I'm glad I got to you in time."

"Me, too." She brought his hand to her cheek and smiled.

An ache exploded in his chest. She could have been hurt

or even killed. He slipped his hand from hers. "I'll flag down emergency. Stay put."

"Yes, Chief."

Nate stood, waving down the ambulance and squad car. Maddie, Cassie's cousin and a local EMT, came bounding toward them.

"Cassie?"

"She's okay."

She noticed Nate's wound. "Whoa, what about you?"

"I'm fine. Take care of your cousin."

Detective Vaughn screeched to a stop and flung open her car door. She marched toward Nate.

"Tony Miller took Cassie at gunpoint," he said.

"Where was he taking her?"

"Not sure, something about meeting a guy that would help find Becca."

"You want me to question her?"

"No, I'll take care of Cassie. I need you to figure out what they want from her. She received a threatening call at the resort."

Nate's phone vibrated, but he didn't recognize the number. "Chief Walsh."

"It's Agent Nance. I have some information to discuss with you."

"I'll send Detective Vaughn."

"I'd rather speak with you."

Nate wanted Detective Vaughn to take the lead so Nate could protect Cassie. But he was police chief and couldn't shirk his duties.

"Meet me at Healthy Eats in an hour," Nate said.

"Will do."

Nate ended the call and studied his phone.

"Who was that?" Vaughn asked.

"FBI agent wants to meet." He glanced back at Tony's car. Maddie was checking Cassie's vitals. Cassie smiled at Nate.

"Want me to meet with the Fed?" Detective Vaughn said.
"Actually, we're all going."

An hour later Nate and Detective Vaughn were seated
across a booth from Agent Nance, while Cassie hid in the
kitchen. That was the best way to keep her safe: make her
invisible.

Nate's sister, Catherine, owner of Healthy Eats, was
happy to brew them a pot of coffee after closing. Not that
they'd stay long. Nate wanted the meeting with Nance to be
quick so he could take Cassie someplace safe.

"That's what we suspect," Agent Nance said. "The Sar-
tuchi family is smuggling their guys, who are out on bail,
out of the country by way of Echo Mountain, Washington."

"Why here of all the places in the country?" Nate said.

"Haven't figured that out yet."

"Well, figure faster, people are getting hurt," Detective
Vaughn shot back.

Agent Nance narrowed his eyes at her. "Did I do something to offend you?"

"Smuggling, how?" Nate redirected before Vaughn and
the agent got into a shouting match.

"We think they hide out in the cabins for a week or
two where they're given passports for their new identities,
money and plane tickets," Agent Nance continued.

"But Sea-Tac airport is two hours away," Detective
Vaughn said.

"They could take the airport bus," Nate offered. "For that
matter, they could take a bus north into Canada."

"Whatever the case," Agent Nance continued, "we think
they book lodging through Echo Mountain Rentals, and
Becca Edwards and Tony Miller were hiding the passports
and money in the cabins."

"Becca Edwards has no criminal record, and her em-
ployers say she's a hard worker," Detective Vaughn said.

"Yet she's disappeared and her boyfriend took Cassie

McBride hostage," Agent Nance countered. "Where is Cassie, anyway?"

"Safe," Nate said.

"She could be our best leverage to get Len Pragner to talk."

Nate didn't like the sound of that.

"How do you figure? She didn't see him commit the murder," Nate said.

"No, but she can put him at the scene." Nance leaned back in the booth. "I could take her off your hands, put her in federal custody to protect her, and give you time to work the murder case."

That wasn't happening. Before Nate could say so, Vaughn spoke up.

"How is Marilyn Brandenburg, the dead woman Cassie found in the tub, involved in this?"

"We've found no connection between her and the mob." Agent Nance glanced at Nate. "I was hoping you could share what you've got so far. Maybe we can piece together some answers."

Nate nodded at Detective Vaughn. "Go ahead."

"Marilyn was a nurse from Moscow, Idaho. Worked at Pullman Regional Hospital. Her sister said she wanted a little time away in the mountains. She'd been stressed out at work. She's divorced, kids are grown and married. She's squeaky clean, so why kill her?"

"Maybe she came across something at work?" Agent Nance said.

"She's a pediatric nurse," Vaughn countered.

"We're not going to solve this tonight," Nate said. "We appreciate you filling us in, and we'll give you information on the case as it develops."

"Becca and Tony could be the key to shutting this thing down and sending these guys away for serious jail time," Agent Nance said.

"So let's work together and make that happen," Nate said.

Agent Nance slipped out of the booth. "I'm getting a to-go coffee. Want one?" he asked Nate.

"Sure, thanks."

The FBI agent crossed the room to the coffee station and grabbed a few cups from the counter.

"He didn't offer to get me a coffee," Detective Vaughn said, crossing her arms over her chest.

"You don't drink coffee," Nate countered. "What do you make of all this?"

"Something feels seriously off."

"Agreed. For now, I'm taking Cassie someplace safe. I'll call Chief Washburn back in to help out."

"You sure you wanna do that? It might look like—"

"I don't care how it looks. Having his experience on the team is invaluable. This kind of thing shouldn't be happening in our town."

"No kidding," she said softly.

"I'll fill in Chief Washburn. His presence will keep people calm. You need to find Becca. Pull Red off patrol if you have to. I know he's been wanting to do more detective work."

"Will do. And the Marilyn Brandenburg murder?"

"Keep on forensics for results. Dig into her past. If she's involved, there's got to be a trail. I'll have the chief do background on Len. If he's a mob enforcer, we could use that to help the ADA build a case against him."

Agent Nance returned to the table with the coffees.

"Thanks." Nate got out of the booth and shook the agent's hand. "I'll be in touch."

"Sounds good." With a curt nod at Detective Vaughn, Agent Nance left the restaurant.

Vaughn frowned. "I don't trust him."

"Go home and get some sleep."

"What about you? I could relieve you at three a.m."

"No, I need one of us functioning on a full night's sleep.

I'll conference call with you and Chief Washburn tomorrow morning at eight."

"You got it, Chief."

As Nate drove away from the restaurant, Cassie noticed how tired and defeated he looked, which only made her more determined to figure out a solution to this mess. It wasn't even her mess; it was obviously a mess of Tony's making, and he'd put Cassie's friend in danger.

"It was nice of Catherine to lend you her son's car so no one would recognize us," she said.

"Yep."

"Did it go well with the FBI agent?" she asked.

"Well enough."

She wanted to be a part of the investigation, to help solve the mystery of the dead woman and demanding stalkers. But it seemed like Nate wasn't up to more than one- or two-word answers. He kept checking the rearview mirror to make sure they weren't being followed.

"Did the agent have information about Tony?" she asked.

"Some." He took a sip of coffee.

"Can you share?"

"Tomorrow."

"Well, I could tell you what Tony said about getting into a mess because he didn't think they'd—"

"Cassie, save it until we get there, okay?"

"To the resort?"

"No, a safe house."

"Can you at least tell me who Tony and Becca got involved with?"

He shot her a quick glance. "We suspect this is mob-related."

"Wait, what, here? In Echo Mountain?"

He nodded. "Which is why we need to stay off everyone's radar. Be invisible for a few days."

"That's crazy. I mean there's like no crime in Echo

Mountain. It's a nice town with good people and charming little shops."

She felt suddenly embarrassed by her chatty nature. The poor guy needed quiet, needed to think, yet he was stuck with Cassie, jabber-jawing like a teenager.

She stretched her neck and closed her eyes. She'd be sore tomorrow from the car collision with the tree. Wherever Nate was taking her, she hoped it had a soft bed. A good night's sleep would certainly put her in a better frame of mind to piece things together. She'd start with Tony's comments, and then consider Becca's stressed behavior as of late, and rack her brain for anything she might have in her possession that didn't belong to her.

The car suddenly swerved and her eyes popped open. "Whoa." Gripping the dashboard, she glanced at Nate.

His eyes kept opening and closing, like he couldn't stay awake.

"Nate?"

"Sorry, I'm… I'm—"

A horn blared.

She glanced out the front window and was blinded by headlights of an oncoming car.

ELEVEN

Cassie instinctively grabbed the wheel and yanked it right to steer them out of the path of the car. Nate must have snapped out of his fog because he hit the brakes and the car swerved, coming to a stop on the shoulder.

Cassie shoved the car in Park and caught her breath. Then she leaned over and examined Nate. It looked like his wound had bled through his bandage.

"Nate, your arm." She glanced up. He seemed to be drifting in and out of consciousness. Could it be from blood loss?

"Nate? Nate, can you hear me?" she said.

"Cassie," he said, his voice weak.

A kind of determination shot through her that she didn't know existed, determination that would give her strength to get help for Nate and protect them from the mysterious threat.

She glanced out the back window. The driver of the vehicle that almost hit them was gone.

Nate said they needed to be invisible, which meant she shouldn't call 911 because an ambulance would transport them to the hospital, a very public place.

She hit the hazard lights so they'd be visible to motorists on the dark road, and then plucked his phone out of the holder on the dashboard. With unusual calm, she scrolled through his contacts. She spotted Dr. Spencer's number and made the call, holding her breath.

"Hey, buddy, I heard you were in a gunfight," he answered.

"It's Cassie," she said. "I need your help. Nate is semiconscious and needs medical attention."

"I'll send an ambulance."

"No, we have to stay under the radar because they think the

mob is somehow tied to all this and…and…" She composed herself. "We need to hide out where no one will find us."

"What's his condition?"

"Groggy, drifting in and out of consciousness, and he's bleeding through his bandage."

"Where are you?"

"Highway Two, about five minutes north of Healthy Eats."

"My cabin is ten miles northwest of your location. Take Highway Two four miles and turn left on Rushing River Drive. Follow that until it becomes a one-lane road, then look for the rooster mailbox and turn left. That's my driveway. I'll meet you there as soon as I can."

"You're not home?"

"At the hospital. I'll leave right away. Is his wound seeping or oozing?"

She carefully pulled his jacket down off his shoulder and eyed the dressing. "It seems to be seeping through his bandage."

"Okay, meet me at the cabin."

"Thanks." She shifted Nate's jacket back on and placed her palm against his cheek. "Hey, you'll be okay."

"Cassie," he muttered. "Gotta keep her safe."

"We're safe. But I need you to move over. Here, I'll get out and—"

He gripped her hand and his intense green eyes popped open. A chill danced down her spine.

"I have to protect you." His voice cracked.

"You are protecting me. It's all good. Trust me?"

He nodded, his eyes drifting shut. She slipped her hand out of his and went around to the driver's side. She opened the door and knelt beside him. "Nate, I need you to move over, can you do that?"

"Yeah, what?"

"Move to the passenger seat."

He nodded and started to shift across the seat. She was

grateful that the old car had a bench seat or this would be quite challenging.

"That's it," she coached.

He hesitated. "Cassie?"

"I'm here. Move over so I can drive."

A car honked and she jumped, startled. So focused on Nate, she hadn't sensed a motorist pull over on the other side of the highway. She had to pay more attention to her surroundings.

To the potential danger.

The driver lowered his window. He was an older man, in his sixties. She didn't recognize him.

A part of her wondered if he was with the mob, while another part countered that he could be a local. Even if he was, she didn't want him telling stories about a nearly passed-out chief of police. She blocked his view of the front seat.

"Everything okay?" he asked.

"Yes, thank you. We're good."

"I saw the hazard lights so I thought I'd stop, offer to help."

"That was awfully nice of you. My friend suddenly took ill while driving, but we're A-okay." She tried not to sound too forced.

"Are you sure?" He started to get out of his truck.

"Absolutely." With a pleasant smile, she slid behind the wheel of the car, shut and locked the door, and buckled up. Putting the car in gear, she waved at the man and pulled onto the highway. Glancing in the rearview mirror, she watched the Good Samaritan get back into his truck, but he didn't pull away.

Cassie pressed down on the accelerator, wanting to put distance between them. She simply couldn't trust anyone she didn't know, and even some people she did know.

Becca. Cassie still couldn't believe how Becca had fallen under Tony's influence. It started months ago when Becca broke dates with Cassie because Tony wanted Becca to stay home with him. Cassie would never get romantically involved with a controlling man like that, a controlling and potentially criminal man in Becca's case. What kind of trouble had Tony gotten them into?

She eyed the rearview mirror, but there was no one behind her and she could no longer see the Good Samaritan's truck parked on the side of the road. He must have been exactly who he said he was: a motorist who'd stopped to help.

Cassie didn't like feeling suspicious of everyone she encountered. Maybe if Nate had shared more about what he'd learned from the FBI agent that would have given her some solace or peace. But he'd been short with his answers, and now she understood why: he was struggling to stay conscious to fight off whatever was plaguing him. She hoped it wasn't an infection from the bullet wound.

She stopped herself from slipping into panic mode. Her new role was that of protector, not protectee. She had to take care of Nate for a change, and so far she was doing a decent job. They were on their way to meet the doctor who would treat Nate and assess his condition.

"Wait...where are we going?" he said, opening his eyes.

"We're meeting Dr. Spencer."

"No, can't go to the hospital," he said in a panicked voice.

"We're going to his cabin. No one will find us there."

He nodded and leaned back against the seat. A moment later he mumbled, "I had a place, a better place...they wouldn't find you..."

"Shush. I've got this. And you know why?"

He glanced in her direction, his eyes unfocused.

"Because I'm smarter than I look, big guy. And you know how I can prove it?"

He shook his head indicating that he didn't.

"Because I climbed down a mountain with a dog in my arms and hid from creepy Shovel Man."

"Shovel Man," he repeated.

"He might have called out my name, but he didn't know where I'd gone." She tapped her finger against her temple.

"I used my head. Just like I'm doing now. I've got my eye on the rearview to make sure we're not being followed. We're not. And we'll go to Dr. Spencer's cabin for private medical attention. See how smart I am?"

"Y-e-ah," he said, slowly.

She realized by talking to him, she could ease his anxiety. So she'd keep at it.

"You're in good hands, and you don't need to worry about anything. We'll take care of you. I'm just sorry I don't have EMT training like my cousin Maddie. I could have assessed your wound better and maybe even re-dressed it. Then again, I don't have first aid supplies with me. That wouldn't stop Aiden, of course. He was always finding solutions to problems, even as a little kid. Dad called him Mr. Fix-It. I think that's why Aiden's so good at being a resort manager. He knows how to fix things—well, most things. His relationship with his sister? Not so much."

She glanced across the front seat. Nate's eyes were closed. Smiling to herself, she was proud that her nonstop chatter had actually soothed him.

"What happened?" Nate said.

"What do you mean?"

"You stopped talking."

"I thought you were asleep."

"Don't stop."

She smiled and launched into her plans to explore castles in Europe.

Nate drifted. Half awake, half asleep. He wasn't sure what was real and what was a dream. He couldn't remember what day it was, or even where he was.

But he remembered her voice, that sweet, melodic voice of Cassie's that somehow eased the tension from his muscles, and the dread from his thoughts. She talked about castles and islands in Ireland, and cliffs overlooking the

Atlantic Ocean. He drifted, picturing the Irish countryside and the vast ocean.

Then she'd said, *You're okay*, and he went dark, passed out or fell asleep.

Leaving her vulnerable. The sweet girl with a big heart. He'd left her at the mercy of mob thugs. The image of Becca's boot and jacket haunted him. What if they got to Cassie, what if…

"Cassie." He opened his eyes and sat up.

"I'm here."

He glanced to his left and saw her get up from the kitchen table. She was beside him in seconds, placing her warm hand on his shoulder, his bare shoulder. He glanced down at his naked chest.

"How are you feeling, Chief?" Spence asked, coming into view over Cassie's shoulder.

Spence must have taken off Nate's shirt in order to treat his wound. "I… How did I get here?"

"Cassie called me last night with an SOS so I had her meet me at the cabin," Spence said. "Needed to re-dress the wound and check you out."

"I don't remember that," he said.

"You were pretty out of it," she offered.

"I passed out?"

"It's okay," she said. "I got us here. And you even had a good night's sleep."

"Someone could have followed us." He stood and wavered.

"Whoa, take it easy." Spence gripped his arm.

"What time is it?" Nate asked.

"Seven thirty," Cassie said.

"I've got a conference call at eight a.m." He looked around for his shirt.

"Here." Cassie grabbed a throw blanket off the sofa and draped it across his shoulders. She and Spence stayed close as Nate shuffled to the table. With each step he seemed to get his strength back.

He shifted onto a chair and Spence checked his vitals. Cassie grabbed mugs out of a cupboard.

"I'm fine," Nate said to Spence.

"You're not fine or you wouldn't have passed out last night," Cassie said. "Then again, maybe it was my chatter that put you to sleep."

Oh yeah, her melodic voice telling him stories about her family, Aiden's fight with his dad about joining the army, and Bree's decision to move to the city against her parents' wishes.

Nate also remembered a wave of calm washing over him as she chatted away. How was that possible? The answer was too simple to ignore: he was falling for her.

"I'm okay, right, Doc?" Nate asked.

"Your vitals look good this morning. Last night your blood pressure was unusually low, so we took turns keeping an eye on you. You didn't lose that much blood from the bullet wound, and without blood work I can't make an official diagnosis. You could be suffering from exhaustion or dehydration or a combination of both. When was the last time you ate or slept?"

"I haven't seen him do much of either since he rescued me from the mountain ledge," Cassie said.

She slid a bowl of oatmeal in front of him along with a mug of tea. "Drink this." She sat at the table.

"I was hoping for coffee."

"Tea is healthier than coffee."

Nate glanced at Spence for help.

"Sorry, buddy, but I'm not getting in the middle of this," Spence said.

"Not to lecture or anything," Cassie started. "You're great at taking care of everyone else, Chief, but not so much yourself."

"I've been a little busy," he shot back.

"I know, I'm sorry."

"Hey." He reached out and took her hand. "No more apologizing for things that aren't your fault."

"Well, if it weren't for my predicament you'd be sleeping and eating better, that's for sure."

"You're not responsible for what's happening, got it?"

"Yeah, thanks."

He tried releasing her hand, but she wouldn't let go.

"So what is happening, exactly?" she asked. "What did the FBI agent tell you?"

He spent the next twenty minutes going over the details of the case, from the smuggling of bail jumpers, to the suspicion of someone at Echo Mountain Rentals being involved.

Nate respected Cassie's need to know what kind of trouble she'd been pulled into, and it was important that Spence be kept in the loop, especially since he was offering to shelter them from criminals.

"And what about Becca?" Cassie asked.

"No sign of her. We found her jacket, a boot, hat, gloves and a scarf up in the mountains."

"Oh, Becca." Cassie interlaced her fingers and closed her eyes.

Nate assumed she was praying for her friend. He bowed his head and waited, wishing he could pray. If he did, it would be for Cassie's safety.

"Amen," she whispered, and looked at Nate. "What happens next? How do we put these guys in jail?"

"The FBI is building a case, but they need witnesses, and we're hoping Becca and Tony would step forward to testify."

"And if they can't find Becca and Tony?"

"You saw Len Pragner at the cabin. You're the best thing they've got to putting him at the scene of the murder."

"But I didn't see anything other than him carrying a shovel."

"They want to use that as leverage."

"Huh," she said.

Nate sensed something was brewing behind her bright blue eyes. "Cassie?"

"I'll get more firewood," Spence offered, probably to give them privacy.

"No, you should hear this, too," Cassie said.

"Hear what?" Nate said.

"I made a decision while you were unconscious last night."

He eyed her. "I have a feeling I'm not going to like this."

"My bad timing will not prevent you from solving this case."

"Bad timing?"

"You know, wrong place, wrong time."

"Cassie—"

"You should be investigating that woman's murder, not babysitting me."

"You're a potential witness to a homicide, and someone is after you because they think you have something that belongs to them. My job is to keep you safe until we solve both the murder and the smuggling operation."

"Well, my new goal is to stop being a victim and help you do just that." She hesitated. "If you're up to it."

"I'm fine."

"Good." She glanced at Spence. "Do you have paper and pens?"

"I think I might have some in the office, hang on." Spence disappeared into a spare room.

She pushed Nate's oatmeal closer to him. "Eat."

"What's with the paper and pens?"

"I'm going to help you do your job."

He started to protest.

"I may seem like a ditz," she said, cutting him off. "I talk too much and act happy all the time. But when I was stuck in bed as a kid, I read anything and everything to help me escape my life. I'm pretty smart, Nate, and I plan to help you solve the murder and find Becca."

Although he was tempted to tell her there was no way he'd allow her to get more involved in these cases, he had to appreciate her enthusiasm.

"I suppose nothing I say will change your mind," he half joked.

"You know me so well. Now eat, or do you need me to feed you?" She reached for the spoon.

"Don't even think about it." He grabbed the spoon and caught her smiling at him. They were sharing a playful moment while embroiled in a crisis.

But he couldn't risk the distraction.

He took a bite of his oatmeal and considered ways of distancing himself without hurting her feelings.

"Who's the call with?" she asked.

He swallowed his oatmeal. "Detective Vaughn and Chief Washburn."

"Chief Washburn? But he's retired."

"I called him in to handle things while I'm out in the field."

"Oh, you don't think, I mean, will that look like—"

"I don't care."

"But you like your job."

He glanced into her eyes, but had no words. What could he say? That he liked his job, but he liked her more? That somehow over the last year her sweet nature had gotten under his skin and he hadn't realized until just today how much he cared about her?

No, he couldn't say any of that.

"The chief's presence will make folks feel safe," he said.

Cassie didn't look convinced.

"I'd better call in." He started to get up, but she stopped him.

"Oh no, you stay right there. And put it on speaker so I can hear."

"I don't think—"

"I won't say a word, promise."

Spence came back into the main living area and placed paper and pens on the kitchen table. "How can I help?"

"When's your next shift?" Nate asked.

"I'm supposed to stop by the urgent care later this morning, but I can find someone to cover."

"No, don't. Continue your normal routine. I don't want to put you in danger because they suspect you're helping us."

"Got it. You two can stay here as long as necessary."

"How many people know about the cabin?" Nate asked.

"Well, you're my first guests, so no one."

"I'm sorry we had to impose on your sanctuary," Cassie offered.

"It's not like that. I just haven't had time for a social life."

Nate sensed there was more to it. Spence was a skilled doctor and a dedicated SAR team member, but he kept his secrets to himself. Nate suspected Spence had experienced some sort of trauma before coming to Echo Mountain that haunted him.

"We appreciate everything you've done for us," Cassie offered.

"Of course." Spence bundled up. "I'm off to get more wood. There's an extra SAR T-shirt for you on the end table." Spence left and the cabin grew oddly quiet.

Nate and Cassie usually seemed comfortable with each other, but for some reason tension stretched between them.

"I charged your phone last night." Cassie went to the counter and grabbed Nate's phone.

"You think of everything."

"I hope so." She placed it in front of him.

"You may not want to hear this call," he said. "If they found Becca—"

"It's okay. I can handle it. I need to help, Nate."

With a nod, he called the station.

"Good morning, Chief," Chief Washburn said.

"Good morning. Is Detective Vaughn with you?"

"Yes, sir," she responded.

"And Cassie McBride is with me," Nate said. "Do we have an update?"

"Got preliminary forensics," Vaughn said.

"That was quick."

"I called in a few favors," Chief Washburn said.

"Thanks."

"Our victim in the cabin died from blunt force trauma, but they found no blood evidence on the shovel to indicate it was the murder weapon. It confirms what we suspected, that she hit her head on the tub," Detective Vaughn started. "Not helpful, I know."

"What about prints?"

"Couldn't find Len Pragner's anywhere. He's in the system so they should have popped pretty quick."

"So we can put him outside the cabin, but not inside," Nate said. "Must have been wearing gloves."

"The thing that bothers me is there's no connection between Marilyn Brandenburg and this whole mob thing," Chief Washburn said.

"Okay, so let's look at this as two completely different crimes: Marilyn's murder, and smuggling bail jumpers out of the country. Vaughn, you've interviewed people in the victim's life. Is there any clear motivation why someone would want her dead?"

"None, sir."

"Maybe she's like me," Cassie interjected, then placed her hand over her mouth.

"Go ahead," Nate encouraged.

"Well, maybe she was in the wrong place at the wrong time. She was late checking out of the cabin and Shovel— I mean Len Pragner was looking for Tony or Becca, but found Marilyn instead. I mean, Becca was originally supposed to be there."

"Which still doesn't explain why Marilyn was murdered," Detective Vaughn said. "Why risk killing a random tourist?"

"Finding Becca and Tony will help us fill in the blanks," Nate said. "Let's focus our efforts in that direction." He glanced at Cassie. "What did Tony say to you in the car?"

"That someone wanted to talk to me and in return that person was going to help Tony get Becca back."

Nate fisted his hand at the thought of Cassie being taken to a meeting with mob thugs.

"Sounds like the mob's got guys in town," Chief Washburn said.

"We have to assume so, yes," Nate said.

"Tony also said something about messing up, that there was so much of it and he didn't think they'd notice?" Cassie offered.

"Now it's making sense," Nate said. "These two were skimming."

"From the mob," Chief Washburn added. "What were they thinking?"

"We have to find them before the mob does," Nate said. "If they haven't already."

"Maybe it's time to enlist the town for help," Chief Washburn said.

"I don't want to cause panic or put innocents in danger," Nate countered.

"It wouldn't hurt to have a few key folks keep an eye on things, let us know about strangers in town," Chief Washburn said.

Nate stood, feeling suddenly like a failure. "It's my job to protect them. I don't want to put them at risk."

"You won't, son. I'm talking about folks like Harvey, and Grace Longfellow of SAR. They always know what's going on in town. It's in their nature."

"If you think they will respect the boundaries and not risk their safety."

"Absolutely," Chief Washburn said.

"Then I trust your judgment," Nate said. "Detective, put out a BOLO on Becca and Tony."

"Yes, sir."

"You keep that young lady safe," Chief Washburn said.

"That's the plan. I'll check in later."

Nate collapsed against the wooden chair. Cassie offered a halfhearted smile. "You didn't finish your oatmeal."

"Lost my appetite."

"Hey." She touched his hand resting on the table. "You're doing the best you can. That's all anyone can ask."

"I've been chief for less than a year and it feels like it's all coming apart on me. You'd think, with my experience, I could get ahead of things."

"No one could have expected something like this to happen in our town. The mob? Come on."

Nate eyed her. "Hang on, you're right."

"I am?"

"There has to be a direct connection between the mob and Echo Mountain." Nate stood and paced to the sofa. He shucked the blanket and put on the long-sleeved shirt Spence had left him. "We need to approach this from a different angle. The mob wouldn't randomly pick Echo Mountain, so what's the connection?"

"That's why I've got pen and paper. We'll write everything down and—"

The front door burst open and Spence hovered in the doorway. "You've gotta get out of here. Now!"

TWELVE

"What happened?" Nate said.

"An SUV is coming up the drive. Take this." He grabbed a jacket off the coatrack by the door and tossed it at Nate. "It will keep you warm in the mountains. Cassie, get my spare pack out of the closet. It's well stocked with food and supplies for a couple days."

Cassie did as ordered, trying not to think about the potential danger headed toward them. She flung her shoulder bag across her body and waited for further instruction.

Spence grabbed car keys off the table. "Let's go."

Cassie handed Nate the backpack, and they rushed out of the cabin.

Once outside, the doctor pointed toward a trail that disappeared behind a cluster of spruce. "The other end of that trail will drop you at the mouth of Lake Serene. You can find your way back to town from there."

Nate gripped his friend's arm. "You're coming with us."

"No, I'll throw them off by driving your car in the opposite direction."

"Spence—"

"Go, I know what I'm doing."

"But—"

"I'll call 911 if I need help. Move it."

As they headed for the trail, Nate glanced over his shoulder.

"I've got this!" Spence called.

Nate shifted Cassie ahead of him and they practically sprinted into the woods. Neither spoke for a good few minutes. Once out of sight, Nate touched her shoulder. "Hang on a sec."

Nate peered through the thick mass of western red cedar and Douglas fir trees to the cabin below.

Cassie looked as well, trying to calm her frantic heart-beat. The SUV slowly rolled up the driveway as if the men inside were deciding the best way to approach the cabin.

"Come on, Spence, get out of there," Nate muttered.

The air seemed colder, crisper, than a minute ago as they anxiously waited to make sure their friend had escaped. The front door to the cabin was still open and Dr. Spencer was nowhere in sight. She automatically dug her fingers into Nate's arm.

The ominous dark SUV stopped at the end of Dr. Spencer's driveway. Was the doctor still inside?

"Call for help," Cassie said to Nate.

"They wouldn't get here in time."

Three men got out of the SUV. One wore a black trench coat that could easily conceal a weapon. They scanned the mountain range, as if looking for Cassie and Nate.

"Hang on," Nate said. "I recognize one of those guys from Becca's tour group. The one with the ski cap."

The obvious leader in the trench coat said something to the other men. They approached the cabin.

"I need to help Spence," Nate said.

Panic shot through Cassie's body. "He said he had a plan." She was desperate not to lose Nate to these violent men.

He took her hands in his and looked into her eyes. "Cassie, I can't abandon my friend."

She nodded, understanding that guilt about his partner's death was driving him to protect the doctor. He leaned forward and kissed her cheek.

It was a goodbye kiss.

"Follow the trail like Spence told you," he said, taking off the backpack. "And don't look back, no matter what you hear, got it?"

She didn't nod this time; she couldn't.

He turned to hike down the trail when Cassie noticed something out of the corner of her eye.

A car speeding away from the cabin.

"Wait, look," she said.

It was Dr. Spencer driving Nate's nephew's car. "He must have been hiding in the car the whole time."

"He was waiting for them to go into the cabin so he could get a head start."

The guy in the trench coat hit the horn and the men scrambled out of the cabin. One got into the car with trench coat man, while the third remained behind.

The SUV took off after Dr. Spencer, just as he'd hoped.

"Why aren't they both going?" Cassie said.

"They can't be sure we're in the car." The third man went into the cabin and shut the door.

"So they're leaving him in case we come back?" Cassie said.

"Looks like." Nate pulled out his phone and called Detective Vaughn. He gave her the make, model and license plate for the car he'd borrowed from his sister. "Spence is driving and he's being pursued by some suspicious-looking men. Get him help. Also, they left one of their guys at the cabin. Yep…we're headed into the mountains, gonna attempt to disappear for a while." Nate pocketed his phone and nodded at Cassie. "All right, let's go."

They hiked for hours, and Cassie figured it was nearly noon when they finally reached Lake Serene. She had been pretty good about monitoring her questions and general chatter. Asking Nate every ten minutes if he was feeling okay wasn't going to make him any healthier, and would probably drive him nutty. Still, she worried about his bullet wound and his energy level.

"We should probably stop for a snack," Nate said.

She touched his jacket sleeve. "Are you tired? Hungry? Dizzy?"

"Cassie." He paused and offered a smile. "I'm fine. But it's been at least four hours since you've eaten. I imagine Dr. Spencer has snacks in his backpack."

He shucked the pack and eyed her. "What's wrong?"

"What do you mean?" Cassie sat down on a nearby rock.

Nate took out a bag of trail mix. "You've been too quiet. Are you worn out from hiking?"

"No, hiking is invigorating."

"But you haven't said much."

"I figured you liked the quiet."

He offered her the trail mix and she dug out a handful.

"I like it quiet, sometimes," he said, scanning their surroundings. "Other times I appreciate the sound of your voice."

"Yeah, it's like background music," she joked.

"It's more than that." He reached over and tipped her chin with a bent forefinger.

"You know I'll do my best to protect you, right?"

"Yes."

With a confident nod, he popped some trail mix into his mouth. They ate in companionable silence. It struck her that she didn't feel the need to jabber away when she was with Nate. Totally comfortable in his presence, she was simply enjoying the fresh air and a moment of peace.

Nate's ringing phone shattered the serenity.

"Detective?" he answered, then frowned. "I see." He stood and took a few steps toward the lake.

Cassie wondered if he didn't want her hearing details about the case. Bad news, perhaps? As she watched him pace back and forth, she realized he was frustrated.

"I'm not sure yet. Our goal was to make it to Lake Serene… Yes. Thanks." He glanced at Cassie. "They lost track of the car following Spence, but he's okay."

"You don't sound happy."

"I shouldn't have let him lure those guys away like that. It put him in the eye of the storm."

"It was his idea, and he's okay, right?"

Nate nodded. "He took the risk because he wanted us to

be safe, so we should keep going." She picked up the backpack, but Nate took it away from her.

"I got it."

"Your wound—"

"It's fine." He strapped on the pack and motioned her ahead.

The trail was wide enough that they could walk side by side, a good thing since she sensed he needed to talk.

"What's the plan, Chief?" she said.

"Find temporary shelter until we can get to the safe house, which has been a challenge. I still can't figure out how they found us at Spence's cabin."

"Speaking of temporary shelter, I have an idea. Echo Mountain Rentals has a few properties under construction. What if we stayed in one of those?"

"But the work crews—"

"Construction is on hold for two of the cabins due to some kind of contract issue or something, I don't know the details. The properties are sitting vacant. I think the closest one is Horizon Point."

"How far?"

"I'm guessing about three miles east of here? Let me check the map." Nate hesitated and she dug it out of the side pocket of the pack. "Yep, here it is. Actually, we might be able to avoid major roads and cut through here." She pointed to a trail. She folded the map. "We should probably notify Mr. Anderson so no one calls the police on us."

"Not a good idea. I don't know who I can trust."

"Mr. Anderson's a good guy, a little scattered, but that's why he has Carol."

"Yet she couldn't keep the personnel files safely locked."

"We all make mistakes. Even you," she teased.

Nate didn't smile and seemed to fall into deep thought. She wondered if he was still beating himself up about Dr. Spencer.

Rather than try to talk him out of his self-recrimination,

Cassie silently asked God to lighten the burden from his heart. He was such a good, kind man, a man who could seem impenetrable on the outside, but she knew he was gentle on the inside. He didn't deserve to suffer.

"I know what you're doing," he said.

"Excuse me?"

"You're praying for me, aren't you?"

"What if I am?" She glanced sideways at him.

"I guess—" he hesitated "—I'd say, thank you."

"You're welcome."

They continued along the trail, Cassie pleased that he appreciated her prayers. Silence once again stretched between them like a line connecting a boat to a buoy. Even in silence they'd become close. She never imagined that could happen, especially with a man like Nate.

"I've been negligent," Nate suddenly said.

"What do you mean?"

"With God. Actually, I've been without God since, well, I'm not sure I've ever had a relationship like that."

"God is always there for you, Nate. 'An ever-present help in trouble,' according to the Bible."

She took his hand, thinking the contact might make him feel less alone, less distanced from both her and the Lord.

"You are…remarkable," he said, squeezing her hand.

In that moment she felt something much stronger than friendship blossoming between them, and it wasn't one-sided on her part. Could it be that a life-threatening crisis had brought them together and made them realize they had feelings for each other? The corners of his lips raised slightly as he glanced at her.

Sudden movement caught her eye over his shoulder. Before she could register what was happening, a man hurled himself out of nowhere at Nate.

"No!" she cried.

Nate automatically pushed her aside and whipped around as the attacker slammed into him. The men hit the ground and rolled a few times, the guttural sounds sending shivers down her arms. The awkward pack put Nate at a disadvantage.

Cassie scanned the immediate area looking for a weapon and spotted a thick branch a few feet away. But could she use it on the attacker? The guy, in his forties wearing a blue knit cap, wrapped his arm around Nate's neck and strangled him from behind.

"Let him go!" she shouted.

The man tightened his grip. Nate swung his arms, trying to break free.

The guy jerked his arm again.

Nate's legs buckled.

Both men went down.

"God forgive me," she whispered.

She grabbed the branch, about the length of a baseball bat, and swung, hitting the man in the back.

He jerked in response, but didn't let go of Nate.

She was not going to watch a criminal murder Nate.

The love of her life.

"I said, let go!" she warned.

The guy squeezed tighter. Nate's arms went limp by his sides. Complete and utter panic drove her to swing the branch again and again. The third swing connected with the guy's head.

He suddenly let go of Nate and stumbled to his feet. Nate rolled onto his side, coughing and gasping for air.

He was alive. She sighed with relief.

The attacker took a step toward her, his eyes flaring with rage.

She fought back paralyzing fear and considered her next move. Much bigger than her five-foot-three-inch frame, the guy could easily take away the branch and even use it on her. Yet she knew they didn't want her dead because they thought she had something of theirs.

"Stay away," she threatened, clinging to the branch.

She just needed to buy enough time for Nate to regain his strength.

The man took another step toward her.

She was not a defenseless woman. She'd taken a self-defense class with her sister, Bree, when she'd returned to Echo Mountain.

He took another step.

"What do you want?" she demanded.

A sinister smile eased across his lips.

He stepped closer.

She jabbed the branch at his crotch. He instinctively pitched forward to protect himself and she swung the branch, hard, nailing him on the side of the head.

He collapsed, seemingly dazed. She stood there for a few seconds, heart pounding in her ears, a little dizzy from the adrenaline rush.

Cassie scrambled to Nate. "Are you okay?"

"Yeah."

The attacker moaned.

Adrenaline reignited her body. She grabbed Nate's gun out of his holster and aimed at the guy.

"Don't move!" she threatened, even though she didn't know much about guns and the safety was probably still in place.

The guy went still, either because she'd threatened him or because he was unconscious.

She glared down the barrel of the weapon, hoping the threat of being shot would be enough to keep him from coming after her or Nate.

"Cassie," Nate said, his voice hoarse.

She couldn't speak. Couldn't even form words. A metallic taste filled her mouth. She could see her hands trembling as they gripped the gun, but she was not letting go.

Had to protect Nate. He'd been hurt enough.

"Cassie."

She felt Nate's hand touch her shoulder from behind, then slide down her arm. "It's okay. Release the gun."

With gentle pressure, he eased her arm down so she was no longer aiming at their attacker.

"Let go," he said.

She nodded, but her fingers were locked in place, like they were glued to the cool metal.

"It's okay," he whispered against her ear.

The warmth of his breath filtered down her arm, easing the tension from her fingers.

"That's it, just relax."

A burst of air escaped her lips. She'd been holding her breath.

"Shh, you're doing great," Nate coached.

She willed herself to unclench the gun, but it was like someone else's hand was attached to her body.

Nate wrapped his fingers around her hand. His warm palm blanketed her knuckles and seemed to melt her frozen joints. She stretched her fingers, releasing the gun. Nate eased it out of her grip.

"That's it," he hushed.

"I... I was protecting you."

"Yes, you were. And you did an excellent job."

Nate steadied his hand as he retrieved the gun from Cassie, not wanting her to see that he was shaking, as well. She might be trembling from the adrenaline rush of violence, but Nate's body trembled from the lack of oxygen. He'd almost been strangled to death.

In front of Cassie.

He'd been distracted by her beauty and kindness, and had almost gotten them both killed. Well, Nate would have been killed. It was pretty clear they wouldn't kill Cassie until they got answers.

"Are you okay?" he asked, his lips touching her soft blond hair.

"Yes."

He aimed the gun at their motionless attacker, the guy from Becca's tour group. It never should have gotten this far. Cassie shouldn't have been put in the position of having to shoot a man. The trauma of wounding or killing another human being would have stayed with her forever.

Changed her forever.

It was Nate's fault. He'd drifted into a false sense of security out here in the wilderness while looking into her expressive blue eyes.

Nate approached their attacker. Blood trailed down the side of the man's head. Nate nudged him with his boot, but the guy didn't respond. He knelt and pressed the barrel of the gun against the guy's forehead.

"I will pull the trigger if you make a move," he warned.

Again, no response.

Nate pressed two fingers against the man's neck to feel for a pulse.

"Is he… Did I?" Cassie uttered in a shaky voice.

"He's alive. Can you go into the backpack and find a first aid kit and some rope?"

When she didn't move, Nate glanced at her. Eyes wide, she continued to stare at the wounded man. It was as if she had just awakened from a dream and realized what she'd done, that she'd inflicted the head injury and caused all the blood.

"Rope and first aid?" he prompted in a firm tone.

Her gaze shot up to meet his. "Oh, right."

She dug into Spence's backpack, strapped to Nate's back. A moment later she handed him rope.

"You need to bind his wrists." With the gun still pointed at the guy, Nate rolled him onto his stomach.

Cassie pulled his wrists behind his back and bound them as tightly as she could. Nate holstered his gun and pulled the knot even tighter.

Nate used remaining rope to secure the man to a nearby tree, where he assessed his injuries.

"Head wound doesn't look too serious." Nate wiped the gash clean and applied a bandage. "That's all we can do for him. We'd better go. He may not be alone." Nate packed up the supplies.

"We…leave him here?"

"Yes, but I'll get him help." Nate led Cassie away and called in. "This is Chief Walsh. I need a law enforcement team to retrieve a suspect, midforties, just north of Lake Serene on the trail. He's tied to a tree and unconscious. I administered first aid, but he's dangerous. Proceed with caution, over."

Cassie glanced at their attacker. "He was going to kill you."

Nate put his arm around her, hoping to ease her anxiety. She didn't push away, yet he felt her body stiffen.

He let his arm slide off her shoulder and they walked in silence. It was a different kind of silence than before. He felt like he was losing her somehow.

Hours later, utterly exhausted by the day's journey hiking through the mountains, Cassie was starting to feel weak for the first time in many years. She fought anxiety about her condition possibly flaring up. These could be normal aches and pains, nothing related to the autoimmune disease that plagued her as a child.

Don't give in to the fear, she told herself.

Not so easy.

Nate would start a conversation with her, probably because she was too quiet, and she'd struggle to find the strength for small talk.

That jerk almost killed Nate.

Right in front of her.

She shuddered at the memory of Nate's arms going limp.

"Cassie," Nate started. "Next time someone comes after me, promise you'll take off and find a safe place to hide."

"I can't make that promise."

"Look." He stopped and gripped her arms. "If I die trying to protect you, I'd like some peace of mind that at least I saved your life. Promise me you'll put yourself first."

There was desperation in his serious green eyes, and pain. Lots of pain.

"Okay, okay." She glanced away and he released her.

After hiking in awkward silence for another half an hour, she spotted the cabin. "There." She pointed to the one-story rental in the clearing below, with a gravel driveway and wooden porch.

As she started down the trail, Nate blocked her. "I'll go first. You stay back until I signal that it's safe."

"No," she said.

"Cassie—"

"You would have been killed if I hadn't been with you. We stick together, Nate. We're better together."

She walked around him, realizing she'd never been that direct with anyone in her life. Maybe it was exhaustion. Maybe it was hunger.

Or maybe she'd finally found her voice.

"Hey, hey," he said, catching up to her. "I'm just trying to keep you safe."

"I know, and I appreciate that."

"But?"

"I guess I'm hungry and tired."

"There's dehydrated food in the pack. We can heat that up for dinner."

Twilight illuminated the property as they approached the cabin. Cassie punched in the override code that unlocked all property doors.

"At least let me go in first," Nate said.

She stepped aside, understanding his need to take the

lead. He placed the backpack on the porch, turned the door handle and went inside.

The door slowly eased shut behind him.

Cassie put her hand on the heavy oak to keep it open.

And saw something come down against Nate's head from behind.

THIRTEEN

Cassie snapped her hand back in shock.

The door clicked shut.

Heart pounding, she darted to the side of the cabin, spotted a small shed and ducked inside. It was her instinct to run, find safety and regroup. She could call for help, but they wouldn't get here in time to do any good. No, she was on her own.

Nate would want her to flee, hike to safety. He'd made her promise to leave him behind.

A light sparkled through the crack in the shed door. Someone was searching the area with a flashlight. And he was headed in her direction. Cassie dug into her bag for keys.

The ball of light grew bigger, brighter.

Her fingers touched a small canister of pepper spray Bree had given her. She calmed her frantic heartbeat and waited for the door to open.

God give me strength.

She blinked to clear her vision.

It seemed like it was taking forever for the guy to find her.

"Who's in there?" a woman demanded.

Cassie recognized that voice.

"Becca?" Cassie flung open the shed door.

Becca lowered a two-by-four she had been gripping as a weapon. "Cassie?"

She threw her arms around Cassie and gave her a hug. Cassie hugged her back, although she still gripped the pepper spray and keys.

Becca released her. "What are you doing here? It's dangerous, a man—"

"Nate." Cassie took off for the house.

"Cassie, don't! There's a guy—"

"Nate Walsh! It's the police chief!" Cassie called over her shoulder. She raced into the cabin and froze at the sight of Nate, unconscious on the floor. Dropping to her knees beside him, Cassie said, "Nate, can you hear me? Come on, open your eyes."

Footsteps pounded on the porch and Becca rushed up behind Cassie.

"I didn't see him, Cassie, I didn't know who it was. Honest, I never would have—"

"What'd you hit him with?"

"A two-by-four."

Cassie ran her hand across the side of Nate's head. "Go get the backpack on the porch. Quick!"

Becca dashed out of the cabin.

"Nate, can you hear me?"

When he didn't respond, she stroked her thumb across his cheek. "You'll be okay. You have to be okay," she whispered. "Ya know why? Because I love you. I've never loved anyone like this before, so could you open your eyes, please?" She waited. "Not yet, huh? Okay, take your time."

As she stroked his hair, she prayed for him to open his green eyes and speak her name.

"I got it," Becca said.

"There should be a cold pack in there, and ibuprofen. Is the water working?"

"No, and no electric. But I have some water left. And there's a creek behind the property. We can get water there if there's a filter in that pack."

"I'm assuming there is."

Becca handed Cassie the cold pack and knelt beside her. Cassie twisted the package, releasing the chemicals, and placed it against the bump on Nate's head.

"I didn't mean it, Cassie. I never would have hit the chief."

"It's okay, he'll understand."

"No, he won't." Becca shot to her feet. "I'm already in trouble because of Tony. He said we weren't doing anything wrong, but now these guys are after me, and I think Tony's working for them and—" she paused "—I don't want to go to jail!"

"Take a breath," Cassie said. "One thing at a time. Help me make him comfortable."

Becca glanced from Cassie to Nate back to Cassie.

"Find me something to prop up his head," Cassie ordered, shifting Nate onto his back.

Becca pulled a pair of jeans out of her backpack, rolled them up and handed them to Cassie. Cassie slipped them beneath Nate's head and readjusted the cold pack. "If he doesn't wake up in a few minutes I'm calling 911."

"No, those men...they'll find us, they'll kill us," Becca said.

"I won't risk Nate's life. If this is more serious than a minor concussion, we'll have to get him to the hospital."

Becca stared in horror at Nate, her eyes widening.

"I need you to tell me what's going on," Cassie said. "Who's after you and why?"

"I can't." She stood and paced to the kitchen sink.

"Really? Because you've dragged me into this violent mess and I don't appreciate it."

Becca spun around. "What do you mean?"

"They think I have something of theirs. What?"

Becca shook her head and put out her hand. "The less you know the better."

"It sounds like Tony is into something dangerous, criminal even. I want you to explain how a good person like yourself could end up going down this path."

"I love him," she said in a hushed voice. Becca's gaze drifted to the floor. "He was always so nice to me, made me feel special...and loved. He brought me flowers for no reason." She glanced at Cassie. "I'm an idiot, right?"

"No." Cassie sighed. "But you need to fix this."

"It's impossible. They're everywhere."

"Is that why you disappeared from the tour group?"

She nodded affirmative. "A guy pulled me aside and said if I didn't tell him where the money was, he was going to kill me before we got down off the mountain. Cassie, we're in so much trouble." Becca burst into tears.

Cassie felt bad for her friend, but was also angry at the decisions she'd made. Becca should have gone to the police and asked for help. Instead she was hiding out in an abandoned cabin.

"What was the plan?" Cassie asked. "Hide out here until when?"

"I don't know. I hadn't thought past getting away."

"You left your jacket and a bunch of other stuff on the trail. Why, to throw everyone off?"

"I needed the men who were after me to think I was dead."

"No, what you need to do is end this before more people get hurt."

Nate moaned and blinked his eyes open. "Cassie?"

"Hey, you're awake. How do you feel?"

"Like I was hit by a truck." He glanced around the room. "What happened?"

"Misunderstanding. Becca thought you were one of the bad guys."

Becca stepped into his line of vision. "I'm so sorry, Chief. Please don't arrest me. I had no idea it was you."

"We thought you'd been kidnapped." Nate struggled to sit up and Cassie helped him. He clenched his jaw as she held the cold pack against his head.

"I was scared," Becca explained.

"The federal authorities would like to speak with you," Nate said.

"Oh my God, am I going to jail?"

Nate stood and Cassie led him to a chair beside a worktable in the kitchen.

"That depends," Nate said. "Have you broken the law?"

"I don't think so, I don't know. I'm stupid. I trusted Tony."

"Well, try trusting me instead. Tell me what's going on."

"I can't, don't you get it? It'll put you in danger."

"In case you haven't noticed, we're already in danger," Cassie shot back. "Tell the chief everything."

Becca sighed and hugged herself.

Cassie stood beside Nate, her hand resting protectively on his shoulder.

"From the beginning," Nate encouraged.

Becca joined them at the table. "Tony worked part-time for Echo Mountain Rentals, dropping things off for guests and taking the laundry in, picking it up, that sort of thing. One day a man approached him and said he was a small businessman wanting to grow his company."

"What kind of business?" Nate asked.

"Laundry services. Tony tells the guy he should talk to Mr. Anderson. The guy says he'll have a better chance if he gets Tony's support." Becca sighed and shook her head. "That should have been his first clue, because Mr. Anderson doesn't take business advice from Tony."

"Continue," Nate said.

"The guy says he's going to offer a lower rate than the current service. But it's a longer drive to his facility, so he's afraid Mr. Anderson won't consider him. If Tony agrees to make the extra thirty-minute drive, the man will pay him a $500 finder's fee. Then, every time he has to make the drive, which is two to three times a week, Tony will get an extra $100 cash. That would certainly pay for the extra gas, plus his time. That's like $300 a week."

"And Tony didn't suspect anything strange about this?" Nate asked.

"No, the man seemed genuine, at least in Tony's opinion, and he needed the money because he was working limited hours for Echo Mountain Rentals. Mr. Anderson is kind of cheap that way."

"Okay, so Tony was driving the laundry to where?" Nate asked.

"A facility near Mount Vernon. He'd drop off the dirty bags of laundry and pick up the nicely packaged clean linens, take them to the office where Cassie and I would pick them up and deliver to the cabins."

"But something changed," Nate said.

"One day, Tony was in a hurry, and a clean linen package ripped." Becca's eyes grew wide as she retold the story. "All his stuff spilled out, like passports and cash, lots of cash."

"That's when he should have called the police, Bec," Cassie said.

"I know, but he didn't. He brought the linens to my place. We didn't know what to do at first, but Tony couldn't resist. He took a hundred dollars cash and we bundled the linen back up, nice and neat. A week later, when no one said anything, he assumed they hadn't noticed."

"Could he honestly be that naive to think it wouldn't catch up to him?" Nate said.

Becca leaned back in her chair. "It's not his fault. He never got a fair shake in life, being orphaned and sent to live with an aunt and uncle who didn't have time for him, and then being expelled from school for no good reason."

"He sounds like he suffers from victim mentality," Cassie said.

"He hasn't had it easy, Cassie."

"We all have our struggles."

"Says the girl with the perfect family," Becca shot back.

Cassie didn't respond. Comparing personal trauma was counterproductive. Nate placed his hand over Cassie's and gave it a squeeze.

"Sorry," Becca said. "I shouldn't have said that."

"Back to the laundry," he prompted Becca.

"That's how it started, with a broken package. I didn't

know he continued to take money. After a month, he'd saved over three thousand dollars between his driving fees and what he was skimming from the packages."

"You had to have known what he was doing, Becca," Cassie said.

"No." She hesitated. "Maybe, I don't know. I suspected, I guess. He kept saying how he was planning this amazing new life for us, because he loved me so much. A few days ago, he shows up at my place with plane tickets to Maui. Said he had a job offer down there and wanted to marry me. We were going to leave right after I brought the group back from the hike. But while I was up there, this guy threatened me. You know the rest."

"You haven't spoken with Tony since you took the group up the mountain?" Nate asked.

"No."

"The man who threatened your life, what did he say?"

"That I wasn't going to make it down the mountain alive unless I told him where the money was." She stood and paced to the window. "Tony said everything was going to be okay."

"He was stealing from the mob," Nate said.

"What?" She turned to them. "No. Tony said it was just some guy moving cash around, you know, because he was being paid under the table for things like fake passports."

"The mob was sending bail jumpers to Echo Mountain Rentals cabins to hide out until they could flee the country with new identities."

Becca came back to the table. "You mean he was helping criminals escape?"

"It looks that way," Nate said.

"And I'm a part of this. I'm going to jail, aren't I?"

"That's yet to be determined," Nate said. "Help us solve this case and you may be able to stay out of jail. There's a federal agent in town who'd like to speak with you."

"What about Tony?"

Nate and Cassie shared a look.

"He's not a bad person," Becca protested. "He didn't know the laundry owner was involved with the mob."

"We'll sort it out once we get safely back to town," Nate said. "It would help to know why they're after Cassie. Any ideas?"

"Because we're friends and they think she knows about the money?"

"What, you mean like I took some of it?" Cassie said.

Becca shrugged. "I guess. I'm truly sorry you got dragged into this."

"Me, too. And I'm sorry you didn't challenge Tony on his activities sooner," Cassie said.

Becca glanced at the floor, ashamed. It was not Cassie's intent to make her feel bad, but she had to face her mistakes.

Cassie's stomach growled. "I'd better eat something before I start gnawing on the table."

"I've got a few cans of hash in my backpack," Becca offered.

"There's dehydrated food in our pack if we can heat up some water," Cassie said.

Cassie and Becca got to work pulling together a meal. They chose the canned items because it would take too long to start a fire outside and heat water.

After eating the last of the cold canned food, Nate said they should rest. He'd take the first watch.

Cassie slept fitfully, if at all, her eyes opening to the image of Nate, her protector, standing guard at the window.

Becca had fallen fast asleep. Well, at least one of them would feel refreshed in the morning. A few hours later Cassie gave up on trying to sleep and went to Nate. "Hey, your turn for some shut-eye."

"You sure?"

"Absolutely. Go on."

"Wake me if you see anything."

"Of course."

Nate brushed a kiss against her cheek and went to lie down on the sleeping bag.

As Cassie kept watch, she thought about everything that had happened in the past few days. Not wanting to be dragged down by fear, she said silent prayers of gratitude: she and Nate were still alive and safe, and they'd found Becca. Plus, Cassie had been able to dig deep down to find the strength to defend Nate from the attacker in the woods.

There was one more thing: Nate had kissed her on the cheek. She smiled to herself.

A few hours later, the early sunrise sparked a sense of peace across the property. She heard rustling behind her. Becca stepped up beside Cassie at the window.

"Did you get any sleep?" Becca whispered.

"Not much."

"Go lie down. I'll keep an eye out."

"Thanks."

"How long has the chief been asleep?"

"A few hours. Wake us if you see anything."

Becca nodded and gazed out the window.

Feeling utterly exhausted, Cassie lay down near Nate. She wished she could reach out and hold his hand, feel his warmth, but sensed it was inappropriate. Yet the ache to touch him made it painfully clear that she'd have to confront him about their relationship at some point.

Something amazing had grown between them, and she planned to hold on to it.

"Cassie?" Becca whispered.

Cassie sat up. "What's wrong?"

"Nothing. I have to go outside for a few minutes." She went to her backpack and took out some tissue. "Be right back."

Cassie lay back down and waited for Becca to return.

And waited.

Something wasn't right.

Cassie got up and started for the door.

The glass window shattered.

FOURTEEN

Nate sat straight up and was about to pull Cassie out of harm's way when she dropped to the floor. He scrambled to her, a ball lodging in his throat.

"Cassie, honey, are you hit?"

She didn't answer at first. He rolled her over, looking into her wide blue eyes.

"I'm okay, but I'm getting seriously tired of this," she snapped.

He pulled her against his chest and hugged her tight.

"Becca," she said against his shoulder.

Nate released her. "She's out there?"

Cassie nodded. Staying low, he made his way to the window and peeked outside, recognizing Tony's hoodie and wild black hair. He shoved Becca into the passenger side of a car.

Nate whipped open the cabin door and withdrew his firearm. "Tony, stop!"

Tony fired off a couple of shots.

Nate dodged back into the cabin. "He's out of his mind shooting at a cop again."

The car screeched as it sped away from the cabin. Nate rushed outside, but was too late. At least he got the make and model, probably another stolen vehicle. Tony was racking up the charges.

"Nate," Cassie called from the cabin.

He holstered his gun and went back inside. She stood at the kitchen table, holding a note in her hand. "It's from Becca. She says she's sorry and begs my forgiveness." Cassie slapped the note on the table. "This is wrong. She wouldn't go willingly with someone so unstable and dangerous."

"I need to alert my team." He called in, giving Detective Vaughn the make and model of the car Tony was driving.

"Wait, he shot at you again?" Vaughn said.

"Yes, add that to the list of charges. This kid is falling fast, and he's got Becca Edwards with him. I'm not sure if she went willingly or not."

"She didn't," Cassie called out.

"We'll find them," Vaughn said.

"Any other developments I should know about?" Nate pressed.

"The guy who attacked you in the mountains yesterday lawyered up."

"Big surprise. Anything more from Len Pragner?"

"Nothing. He's hiding behind his attorney, some guy from Chicago."

"Fantastic," he said, sarcastic.

"What?" Cassie asked, touching his arm.

He glanced into her eyes, realizing how much she trusted him to do the right thing.

"Detective," he said into the phone, "I'm rethinking our current strategy. Our disappearing act is obviously not working, and now Tony knows where we are. If they find him first, it won't take much to pressure Tony into giving up Cassie's whereabouts. I'm bringing her in."

"Yes, sir. Where are you going to keep her?"

"I'll contact Aiden about commandeering Quinn Donovan's fortress apartment at Echo Mountain Resort. If that wing of the resort is empty, it's our most secure location. Also, Becca filled in some of the blanks about the case. We need to be more aggressive in shutting this thing down."

"What have you got in mind?"

"I'll explain it when I see you."

"Want me to send a cruiser to pick you up?"

"Yes. Who's on?"

"McBride and Carrington."

"Send McBride. We're at the Horizon Point property. Have you spoken with Agent Nance this morning?"

"No, sir."

"Once we're set up at the resort I'll want him in on the plan."

"Roger that. Stay safe."

"Thanks." He ended the call and hit speed dial for Aiden.

"My baby sister's driving you nuts, isn't she?" Aiden answered.

"No, actually, she's good. But I need a favor."

"Name it."

"Is Quinn Donovan using his apartment at the resort?"

"He's not expected back for a week. Why, you want to stash my sister there?"

"Yes, if that wing of the resort is mostly vacant."

"I'll relocate the few guests who are there and I'll put extra security on that end of the building."

"Do you need to check with Quinn first?"

"Nah, he gave me blanket permission to use it in case of emergency. I think this qualifies."

"Great, thanks. We'll see you within the hour."

He ended the call but didn't rip his gaze from the property surrounding the cabin. Tony may no longer be a threat, but Nate's adrenaline still hummed just below the surface. For all he knew, Tony could be in direct contact with the mob guys, maybe even told them he'd give up Cassie's location in exchange for Tony's and Becca's freedom.

Which still made no sense—why were mob guys after Cassie? Nate could only assume it was guilt by association.

"I'm so disappointed," Cassie said.

He glanced at her. "I'm sorry."

"Not in you, Nate. You've been amazing. You've been shot, and beat up, and shot at again, and all because my friend fell in love with the wrong guy. I'm so disappointed in Becca."

He refocused out the window. "I think she got that message last night when you challenged the poor decisions she'd made. I was actually quite proud of you."

"You were?"

"Yes, ma'am. You spoke your truth. Not always an easy thing to do."

"I hope that's not what drove her away. I'm upset with her, but I'll always forgive her, even if I don't appreciate being dragged into this, all because of laundry."

Laundry containing passports and cash. That gave him an idea. "Cassie, did you put the clean linen in the Whispering Pines cabin the other night?"

"I didn't have time."

"Which means it's still in your car." He pulled out his phone and called Detective Vaughn.

"Yes, Chief?"

"Cassie McBride's car, I need you to find it and check the trunk."

"What am I looking for?"

"Passports and cash stuffed into linen packages."

"I'm on it, sir."

Nate pocketed his phone. "Now it makes sense. Cassie, how many other rentals did you cover for Becca besides Whispering Pines?"

"Let's see—Hidden Hollow, Serenity Lake and Sunset Vista."

"And each time you delivered a fresh package of laundry?"

"Yes."

"Which you picked up at the office?"

"I did. As a matter of fact, it was weird because some of Becca's packages looked different from the other ones I delivered."

"Did you report that to Mr. Anderson?"

"I mentioned it to Carol and she said she'd check into it, but didn't seem all that concerned. Wait, you don't think Mr. Anderson is involved?"

"We won't know until we do some digging into the mob

connection to Echo Mountain. My gut tells me they didn't randomly choose our town to set up their smuggling operation."

"When we get back to the resort I'd like to help so I can feel like I have some control over my life."

"How about you do internet research?"

"Wow, you didn't say no," she said with a smile.

Nate realized saying *no* to Cassie was becoming harder and harder to do.

They didn't talk for the next half hour and from Nate's expression, Cassie figured he needed quiet time to think and process. She sensed he was upset with himself for the direction of this investigation. Why else would he automatically assume she was disappointed in him?

Or was it something else? Was he withdrawn because somewhere in his unconscious brain he'd heard her confession of love and wasn't sure how do deal with it?

Well if that were the case, they should talk about it, right?

She caught herself. This wasn't the time nor the place to discuss a heady issue like love.

Finally, unable to stand the silence any longer, she approached Nate as he stood guard at the window, waiting for her cousin to show up. She offered a piece of beef jerky. "Breakfast?"

"Thanks."

As he gnawed on the jerky, she followed his gaze out the window to the surrounding property.

"I'm sorry," Nate said.

She snapped her attention to him. "For what?"

"That you had to experience this kind of trauma."

"Well, at least I've got you with me." She looped her arm through his and leaned against his shoulder.

She felt him sigh, and she looked up into his green eyes. "What was that for?"

"What?"

"That heavy sigh."

He shook his head and wouldn't look at her.

"Nate?" She hesitated. "You don't like people keeping things from you, yet you're awfully good at clamming up. It makes people who care about you feel terribly insecure."

"People who care about me," he said in a flat tone.

"Yep, that would be me."

"Well, you shouldn't."

"Too late, and I think you feel the same way. Unless I've been reading your signals all wrong, which I doubt because I've been paying pretty close attention to your body language these past few months. Wait, that makes me sound like a stalker."

Nate pulled his arm free of Cassie's and went to another window.

"I'm not really a stalker," she teased, sensing he was about to shut her out completely.

He snapped his attention to her for a quick second, and the intensity of his eyes was nothing short of alarming.

"Whoa, what was that?" she said.

When he didn't answer, she went to him.

"Nate? You looked at me like…like you hated me."

He stared deeply into her eyes. "I could never hate you."

She felt utterly lost when he looked at her like that. Was this what love felt like? Mature, adult love?

"I hate myself," he spoke so softly she almost didn't think she heard him right.

"What? Why?"

"Because I'm unable to keep you safe, unable to shield you from the brutality of what's going on."

"Hey, you've done a great job protecting me. I'm unharmed and alive."

And in love. For the first time in my adult life.

He ripped his gaze from hers and glanced out the window. "Your cousin's here."

As he started to walk away, she grabbed his arm, stood on tiptoe and brushed her lips against his.

"I'm alive because of you," she said.

When she released him, his brow furrowed like she'd spoken another language, one he didn't understand.

But Nate was a grown man who surely had been in a relationship before.

He had to understand what the kiss meant.

With a tightly clenched jaw, he opened the door and went out to greet her cousin, Officer Ryan McBride. She packed up trail mix and beef jerky, a little dazed by the impact of the kiss. That was awfully forward of her, but it felt right and necessary. She had to let him know there was more to this whole cop-protecting-the-witness thing, a lot more.

Was he so dense that he didn't get it? No, he was purposely dodging the issue, but why? Not because he didn't care about her, because she sensed he did.

At any rate, she'd help with the case because she wanted it solved quickly. Then she could explore her relationship with Nate.

It struck her that she hadn't thought about travel for a while now, not since she and Nate had gone off together, not since he'd challenged her to speak her truth—which she had to Becca.

Thankfully she was getting better at saying what she needed to say with clarity and compassion. The next subject of her honesty would be Nate. If he wouldn't accept the kiss as an indication of her feelings, she'd have to come out and say it: she wanted to date him, explore a future together.

"Wow, can I do that?" she whispered to herself, zipping up the pack.

"Do what?" her cousin Ryan asked from the doorway.

"Um…stay at the resort without Aiden driving me loony birds," she recovered.

"I wouldn't count on it. Come on, coz," Ryan said, shouldering the backpack. "Staying at the resort's gotta be better than being stuck in the wilderness with the silent chief."

Nate cleared his throat from the doorway.

Ryan snapped around. "Ah, sorry, Chief, that's not what it sounded like, sir. I meant the resort is better than being out here with no running water or—"

Nate put up his hand to silence Ryan. "It's fine. Let's go."

"Yes, sir." Ryan rushed out of the cabin.

Cassie glanced around, looking for anything she might have left behind. She grabbed her shoulder bag and marched to the door, hesitating in front of Nate. "Just so you know, we're not done talking."

An hour later they were settled at the secluded apartment on the north side of Echo Mountain Resort. Nate didn't like bringing Cassie, and the trouble that followed her, back to the resort, but the reality was they couldn't get away from whomever was after her no matter how far they went. It seemed as if the mob had eyes and ears everywhere: in the mountains, in town, possibly even in the police department.

No, he was being paranoid. He trusted the former chief with his life, and Detective Vaughn was solid. They were the only two in the inner circle, the only two who knew where Nate and Cassie were at any given moment. At some point Nate had to learn to trust, even if it wasn't second nature to him.

Neither was love.

He'd thought he'd heard Cassie say it back at the Horizon Point cabin when he was struggling to regain consciousness.

She loved him.

Not good for so many reasons.

"Are you talking background checks on everyone in town, Chief?" Detective Vaughn said, standing on the opposite side of the dining room table.

She was speaking to him, discussing strategy, yet he

was so distracted by thoughts about Cassie that he barely heard her.

"Start with anyone associated with Echo Mountain Rentals," Nate said. "That's the hot zone. We also need to track down this mysterious laundry service. It all started with the owner of that company. I want to know who he is, how he got paid and where his facility is located. The Feds can assist with the search of the facility."

"Shouldn't we handle that?" Detective Vaughn said.

"We need to focus on the local angle. Let Agent Nance deal with the mob side of things."

"If he ever shows up," Vaughn shot back. "Oh, and I finally located Cassie's car."

"Finally?" Nate asked.

"There was some confusion. It was towed the other day from Echo Mountain Rentals, but at first no one seemed to know where it ended up. Found it at Rutger's Garage in Lake Stevens, but I haven't had a chance to get down there yet."

"That's half an hour away," Cassie said. "Why did they take it there?"

"Not sure," Detective Vaughn said. "Want me to head there first?"

"No, focus on the new laundry service," Nate said. "See if Mr. Anderson will give you contact information. Agent Nance and I will check on Cassie's car."

"Guys, I think I found something," Cassie said, eyeing a laptop screen.

She was determined to contribute, so Nate had given her an assignment. He'd also given it to her to keep her busy so she wouldn't demand more conversation about their relationship. The time and place for that was after everyone involved in this smuggling operation was behind bars.

"What've you got?" Nate asked Cassie.

"Over the past three months, six men reserved cabins through Echo Mountain Rentals." She glanced up. "But not together and not at the same time."

"They've smuggled six perps out of the country?" Detective Vaughn said. "Were they all originally from the same city?"

"No, actually, different cities across the US, but three from Chicago."

"We need to weed out which ones worked for the mob and which ones were innocent tourists," Nate said.

"I'm on it," Cassie said.

"How are you going to figure that out?" Detective Vaughn asked.

"I'll do searches to see if any of these guys went on hiking trips or local tours. I'm assuming the criminals wouldn't want to be seen in public so their names won't show up on those lists."

"Good point," Vaughn said, and glanced at Nate. "I'm off to talk to Mr. Anderson and track down the laundry service."

"Maybe I should go with you. I can have Agent Nance check out the car."

"No need, Chief," Vaughn said. "I've got this."

"You sure?"

"I'll call if I need backup, promise," she said, and left.

"You're worried about Detective Vaughn," Cassie said.

Nate sat across the table from her. "When I offered her the position of detective I thought she'd be dealing with teenage vandals, not mob criminals. I don't want anything to happen to her."

"Because of Will and the girls?"

Nate nodded. Will had suffered enough after the loss of his wife, and then physical abuse at the hands of white-collar criminals. He'd survived an intense, dangerous situation, and ended up falling in love with Sara Vaughn, a former FBI agent who'd joined the Echo Mountain PD.

Will deserved a little peace. He deserved his happily-ever-after.

"She's a smart cop," Cassie offered. "She'll be okay."

A tap sounded at the door. "That's probably agent

Nance." Nate got up and eyed the peephole. He spotted Cassie's mom, sister and big brother Aiden in the hallway.

"You have company." Nate swung the door wide. "Come on in."

Cassie's mom and sister, holding the little dog, rushed to her side and bombarded Cassie with questions about the last twenty-four hours.

"How's it going?" Aiden asked Nate.

"We're good. Thank Quinn for letting us set up base here."

"Will do. So, have you lost your mind yet?"

"Not yet, but another few days of these guys running around my town and I might."

"I wasn't talking about the case. I was referring to my sister." Aiden nodded toward Cassie. "Nonstop chatterbox, that one."

"Doesn't bother me," Nate said.

"No kidding?" Aiden raised a brow in question.

"She's your sister. You're supposed to get on each other's nerves," Nate said, studying Cassie.

She wore a strained smile she'd never flashed at Nate, a smile that he suspected covered what she was truly feeling. Probably something along the lines of, "leave me alone, you're hovering again."

Another knock sounded at the door and Nate let Officer Ryan McBride into the apartment.

"Whoa, family reunion," McBride muttered.

"Actually, ladies, can I have your attention?" Nate said.

Cassie, her mom and her sister looked up.

"I'm sorry, but we need to keep this visit short. Cassie is doing some work for me on the case. Time is essential if we're going to catch these guys before they come after her again."

"She's helping you?" Cassie's mom said. "Are you sure that's a good idea, Chief?"

"Mom, I'm doing research on the internet," Cassie explained.

"I have to get back to work anyway," Bree said, standing. "I have a strict boss."

"Hey, I let you leave early yesterday for a special date with Scott," Aiden countered.

"A special date?" their mother asked. "What kind of date?"

"Thanks a lot," Bree shot at her brother. "Now she's going to expect us to announce a wedding date."

"Well, shouldn't she?" Aiden pushed.

This is what family looked like, Nate realized. They didn't always agree on everything, and this particular family loved to tease one another. But the love they shared was obvious.

"Can we come back and visit Cassie later, Chief?" her mom asked.

"Yes, but call first. Please be as discreet as possible. These guys could be keeping an eye on your entire family in order to find Cassie. I've got Harvey assigned to you." He nodded at Cassie's mom. "And Scott will stick with Bree when he's off shift."

"Do you know what all this is about?" Bree asked Nate. "What they want from Cassie?"

"We have our suspicions, but I can't discuss details of the investigation at this time."

"Come on, everyone out." Aiden motioned and then eyed his younger cousin Ryan. "You're protecting her, right?"

Officer McBride nodded that he was.

Aiden jabbed a forefinger at Ryan's chest. "Don't mess up."

Once family members had left, Ryan settled at the breakfast bar with a cup of coffee.

"You'll be safe here with Ryan," Nate said to Cassie.

She glanced up from the laptop. "You're leaving?"

"I need to retrieve the laundry from your car. Finding the fake passports will help us track down the suspects."

"But those are new identities."

"Agent Nance can run facial recognition. Speaking of which…" Nate called the agent.

"Nance," he answered.

"It's Chief Walsh. I thought you'd be here by now."

"Rental car broke down."

"Need me to pick you up?"

"Nah, I got another one. Are you at the resort?"

"Yes, but I'm headed to Rutger's Garage in Lake Stevens. Cassie McBride's car is there and I suspect we'll find evidence inside."

"I'll meet you there."

Nate ended the call and glanced at Officer McBride. "I'll be back in a few hours. Keys?"

He handed Nate keys to the patrol car.

"Do not open the door to anyone," Nate reiterated.

"Yes, sir."

Cassie walked Nate to the door. "What else can I do to help?"

Nate hesitated. "Stay safe."

"But is there other research I could do, like—"

Nate pressed his fingertips against her lips, so soft, so perfect. She stopped talking, and her blue eyes widened.

"I can do my job better if I know you're okay." He smiled. "Okay?"

She nodded and gave him a quick hug.

"I'll see you later." Nate glanced through the peephole to make sure the hallway was empty, opened the door and left the apartment.

The burn of worry simmered in his gut as he walked to the squad car. But he couldn't be in two places at once, and he had to trust that between Officer McBride and Aiden watching over her in the fortress apartment, Cassie would be safe, at least until he returned.

Besides, Nate hadn't been all that successful at keeping her safe. It had been one disaster after another up in the mountains, starting with him practically passing out in the car. What was that about? His gunshot wound wasn't that serious and Spence didn't think the bleeding had caused Nate to drift in and out of consciousness.

Well, he was feeling okay now, and ready to take on the men who were terrorizing Cassie. Hopefully he'd find the cash and passports in her car, and get the word out that she was no longer in possession of the items. Then, maybe, they'd leave her alone.

If only it were that easy.

When he arrived at Rutger's Garage, the place looked abandoned. He slowly approached the building, eyeing the closed sign. Closed in the middle of the day?

Nate withdrew his firearm, went to the front door and peered inside. No one was at the counter. He twisted the door handle and found it unlocked. Taking a step into the reception area, he quietly shut the door behind him. A muffled voice echoed from the other side of a closed door a few feet away.

Carefully crossing the small office, he flipped the bolt and flung open the door.

A man rushed out of the closet wielding a broom. Nate pinned him against the front counter.

"I'm a police officer," Nate said, flashing his badge in the guy's face. "Okay?"

The guy nodded. Nate released him. "I'm Chief Walsh from Echo Mountain."

"Cory Rutger," the thirtysomething man said, running a nervous hand through thick red hair. "He had a gun and told us to get in the closet."

"Us?"

"Megan, you can come out," Cory said.

A young woman stepped out of the closet, arms wrapped around her midsection.

"How long ago did this happen?" Nate asked.

"It's hard to say. We were pretty freaked out," Cory said. "Five minutes, maybe ten?"

"It felt like forever in there," Megan whispered.

"Stay here and call 911," Nate ordered.

Nate continued past the counter and looked into the shop where the mechanics worked on cars. It was a small operation, with only three bays. Two of them were occupied, while the third was empty.

And neither of the two cars was Cassie's bright red compact.

"Cory, was there a red VW back there?"

"Yeah, he took the keys to that one."

"So you fixed it?"

"Yep, someone tampered with the ignition pins."

"What did the man look like who took her car?"

"Twenties, black spiked hair."

"Was he alone?" Nate questioned.

"Yes, sir."

"No," Megan said. "I remember seeing him drive up. There was a woman in the passenger seat."

Nate studied the garage. He didn't holster his gun just in case, but suspected Tony got what he wanted: Cassie's car, along with the money and passports.

"You're the only ones here today?" Nate said.

"Yes, sir, my other mechanic is at lunch," Cory said.

"Stay here, please." Nate shouldered open the door into the bay area.

He glanced left, then right. Nothing seemed strange or out of place. Scanning the garage all the way to the back exit, he spotted the car Tony had been driving, and a sedan haphazardly parked, with the driver's door open.

Keeping his back close to the wall, Nate side-stepped tools and cords until he reached the other side of the shop.

Nate studied the sedan parked out back.

Smudges of blood smeared the trunk.

FIFTEEN

Agent Nance was supposed to meet Nate, and the sedan with the open door looked like a rental.

Nate holstered his gun, grabbed a crowbar and rushed to the car.

"Steve," Nate called, leveraging the crowbar against the trunk.

There was no response. Tony wasn't stupid enough to kill or mortally wound a federal agent, was he?

With a quick jerk, Nate opened the trunk.

Agent Steve Nance, bound and gagged, was looking up at him. Nate removed the gag.

"I can't believe that kid," Nance said. "He's going away for a very long time."

"Where are you hurt?"

"Besides my pride?"

"There's blood on the trunk."

"Not mine. His. He was pretty beat up, and that girl looked terrified."

Nate cut the agent free of the duct tape and helped him out of the trunk. "What happened?"

"The girl distracted me, said she needed my help and the next thing I know, I'm on the ground and he's tying me up."

"They took Cassie's car?"

"Yeah, with the evidence."

"At least you're okay." Nate's cell rang. He ripped it off his belt. "Chief Walsh."

"Detective Vaughn ran into trouble at the Echo Mountain Rentals office. I'm en route," Officer Carrington said.

"Ten-four." Nate looked at Agent Nance. "My detective's in trouble."

"Go ahead. I'll give my statement to police and catch up to you."

* * *

By the time Nate reached the rental office, an Echo Mountain cruiser, state patrol car and ambulance were parked in the lot.

Nate got out of his car. The trooper and Red approached him. "She's okay," Red said. "Just a little banged up. She didn't see who hit her."

Nate nodded at the trooper. "Thanks for the backup."

"Sure." The trooper went back to his vehicle.

"Should I hang around, Chief?" Red asked.

"No, go back to your patrol. I'd like to maintain a sense of normalcy in town."

"Yes, sir."

Nate went into the office where Detective Vaughn was being examined by Rocky, along with Cassie's cousin Madeline. Carol the office manager stood in the corner, eyes wide.

"Ma'am, I need to—"

"I'm fine," Detective Vaughn interrupted Rocky, jerking away from him.

Blood dotted her shirt, matted her hair and stained her hands. She glanced at Nate and must have noticed his worried expression.

"Head wounds always bleed a lot. I'm okay, Chief. Thanks to this one." She nodded at Carol who was wringing her hands. "She found me and called it in."

"Carol?" Nate said.

She snapped her attention to him, obviously traumatized by all the blood.

"Thank you for taking care of my officer," he said.

"Oh, uh, sure."

"Why don't you check her for shock," Vaughn ordered Rocky.

"Then you'll come with us?" Rocky said.

"If I have to."

"Oh, she'll go," Madeline said, stepping up to continue the examination of Vaughn's head wound.

Rocky led Carol outside.

"What do you remember?" Nate asked Detective Vaughn.

"Everything, well, until someone whacked me."

Nate noticed a trophy with red smudges on the floor in the corner. He used a tissue to pick it up. "Maybe with this?"

"Probably that Tony punk."

"Couldn't be Tony. He was in Lake Stevens stealing Cassie's car from the garage and tying up Agent Nance."

"Unbelievable," she said, then winced as Madeline tended to her head wound.

Madeline glanced at Nate. "We should take her to the ER."

"Enough." Vaughn batted Madeline's hand away. "I need to talk to the chief alone."

"Give us a minute, Maddie?" he said.

"I'll be right outside." Madeline packed up her supplies and left them alone.

"What did you find?" Nate asked.

"The name and address of the laundry service, Viceroy Laundry, Mount Vernon, plus—" she glanced out the window and back at Nate "—a connection between Mr. Anderson and a Chicago company called Wallingford Imports that I suspect is a front for the mob. I took pictures of email printouts. They're on my phone, but I can't find it."

"We didn't have a warrant anyway. Couldn't use it in court."

"Yeah, but at least we know where to look."

"Speaking of which, how did you end up inside the office?" Nate asked.

"I thought I heard something and climbed in through an unlocked window."

"Heard something?" he challenged.

"A man yelling."

"And when you got inside?"

"No one was here, and the back office was locked. I guess that's where the guy was hiding. Anyway, I did a little, ya know, looking around."

"Which is against procedure. You should have left once you realized no one was in trouble."

"Chief—"

"Pushing the limits is what got you in trouble with the FBI. I told you when I offered you this job that that kind of behavior is not acceptable if you're going to work for me."

She glanced down and sighed. "Sorry, Chief."

Nate would have probably done the same thing if he thought it would give him insight into this case, insight to help him plan a strategy to put these guys away and keep Cassie safe. Still, he didn't want criminals to elude charges because his department hadn't followed proper procedure.

"Come on, you need to get your head looked at by a doctor," he said.

She stood and went white. Nate grabbed her as her legs buckled.

"Madeline!" he called.

She glanced into the office, then called over her shoulder, "Rocky, we need the stretcher!"

Madeline rushed inside and checked Vaughn's vitals. Rocky brought in the stretcher and they secured her in place.

"I'm okay," she said in a strained voice.

Nate fisted his hand in frustration. This had to end.

"Chief, find my phone," Detective Vaughn said as they wheeled her out.

"I will."

Shelving his concern, he refocused on finding the phone. He knelt on the floor and searched under tables and chairs and behind file cabinets. The phone seemed to have disappeared from the tidy office.

The attacker must have taken it with him.

"Chief?"

He stood and glanced at Carol, who hovered in the doorway.

"I was going to lock the office," she said.

"Are you okay to drive?"

"I'm not sure, so I called a car service."

"I could drive you home."

"Thanks, but you've got more important things to do."

"Give me a minute?" Nate searched for Vaughn's phone but with no success. He left the office and Carol locked the door.

"Do you know where Mr. Anderson is?" Nate asked.

"He went to lunch about half an hour ago."

"Have any idea where?"

"No, I'm sorry."

He handed her a business card. "Can you ask him to contact me when you speak with him next?"

"Sure." Eyes downcast, she took the card and walked to a minivan in the parking lot.

Carol would be traumatized by today's events, and it struck him that no one was exempt from the brutality of these criminals, not innocents, not even law enforcement.

Marching to his cruiser, he wondered how he'd tell his friend Will Rankin about Sara's injuries. This was exactly what Nate had been trying to avoid.

He pulled out of the parking lot and called Will on speakerphone.

"Hey, Chief, got a SAR call?" he asked in cheerful voice.

"Actually, I'm calling about Sara."

"What happened?" Will said, his voice suddenly flat.

"She was taken to the hospital with a head injury."

"How serious?"

"She was coherent, but nearly passed out when she tried to stand up. She went into a situation alone—"

"Why didn't you order her to wait for backup? You know she thinks she's some kind of superwoman, but she's not. She's breakable like the rest of us."

"Will, I—"

"I've gotta go."

The line went dead. Okay, that went about as badly as expected.

Nate's next call was to Agent Nance. His voice mail picked up.

"It's Chief Walsh. I'm following a lead at Viceroy Laundry in Mount Vernon. This might be where it all started. Call me back and let me know if you can meet me there."

Nate was about to call Cassie when his phone rang. He thought it might be the FBI agent calling him back. He hit the speakerphone button.

"Chief Walsh."

"Hey, it's Cassie. I wanted to check in. How are you?"

"Frustrated."

"What happened?"

"Tony assaulted the FBI agent and stole your car. Becca was with him."

"What are they thinking?"

"And Detective Vaughn was assaulted."

"Nate, I'm so sorry."

"It's not your fault."

"Are you sure about that?"

"Cassie, let's not go there."

Silence. Then, "I'd better go. Mom and Bree are on the way."

"Be nice," he teased.

"I'm always nice. That's my problem. Talk to you later."

He wanted to call her back, but thought better of it. He knew she was feeling responsible for everything that was happening. Nothing he said could persuade her otherwise.

The best thing Nate could do was chase the Viceroy Laundry lead and gather evidence to end this thing.

"Why did you lie to the chief about your mom and Bree?" her cousin Ryan asked.

"I didn't lie," she said, petting Dasher, who lay content in her lap. "They'll be back shortly, trust me."

"Semantics, coz. What's the deal?"

"I hate putting Nate through this."

Ryan leaned against the kitchen counter, his brows scrunched together. "What are you talking about?"

"Never mind. You wouldn't get it."

"Ya know, not all of the McBride men are thick-skulled, macho types like your brother."

"Uh-huh."

"Maybe I can help?"

"Thanks, but I need to be alone with my thoughts for a while."

"That sounds ominous."

Tapping sounded at the door.

Cassie sighed. "See? Mom and Bree."

Ryan looked through the peephole. "Not quite. It's the FBI agent."

He opened the door and let Agent Nance into the apartment.

"Officer, Cassie," Agent Nance greeted. "Is the chief here?"

"No, he's following up on something. I heard you were assaulted by Tony. I'm so sorry." She sighed and glanced down at the dog.

"Hey." Agent Nance joined her at the dining table. "I'm okay, and we're close to solving this case."

"Not close enough. I can't stand that people are getting hurt because of me."

"Shut up, Cassie," Ryan said.

Agent Nance shot Ryan a disapproving look.

"It's okay," Cassie said to the agent. "He's my cousin."

"Well, he's on duty and should act professionally." Nance nodded at Ryan. "Why don't you take a break?"

"My orders are to stay here, sir."

The agent redirected his attention to Cassie. "None of this is your fault."

"That's what the chief says, too."

Ryan's phone buzzed and he answered, walking into the other room.

"Then believe us," Nance said. "We know what we're talking about."

"I want this violence to end so things can go back to normal."

"Did you feel like Becca was a willing participant, that she knew Tony was stealing money?"

"I'm not sure. I think she got in over her head."

"That's a shame because these guys won't believe that. She's a target, like you. And trust me, Tony and Becca are not smart or resourceful enough to elude them for long."

"You mean…?"

"Whether your friends have the money and passports or not, the mob will put a hit on them."

Cassie closed her eyes.

"But if we bring them in first—"

"It's Bree," Ryan said, rushing up to Cassie. "She's missing."

SIXTEEN

Cassie stood. "Missing, what do you mean missing?"

"They can't find her."

"Scott was supposed to—"

"He got pulled away on a guest emergency, not long, like ten minutes. He's been texting and calling, but she's not responding."

Cassie put the dog down and paced to the door. "I need to find her."

Ryan blocked her. "You're staying here."

"I'll protect Cassie," Agent Nance said. "You go help find your cousin."

Ryan looked from Cassie to the agent, then back to Cassie.

"If you don't go I'll break out of here and search for her myself," Cassie threatened, feeling utterly helpless.

Ryan pointed his index finger at her. "Don't leave this apartment." He whipped open the door.

"Text me when you find her," she called after him.

The door slammed shut. Cassie paced to the sliding patio door, covered by a curtain meant to hide her presence.

"There's got to be something I can do. I can't stand that the people I love keep getting hurt."

"You want to protect them," Agent Nance said.

"More than anything."

"I might be able to help with that. Actually, we'd be helping each other."

Before she could respond, the door opened and Aiden stormed inside. "We're on lockdown. Mom's safe, Scott's out looking for Bree, Officer Carrington is checking out Bree's cottage." Aiden finally noticed Agent Nance standing there. "Where's Ryan?"

"I told him to help find Bree," Cassie said.

"I'll watch your sister," Agent Nance offered.

"What can I do, Aiden?" Cassie asked.

He ran a nervous hand through his thick blond hair. "Nothing, just—" He hesitated. "Don't do anything. Don't call anyone. Just stay out of trouble."

Aiden blew past the agent and left.

Don't do anything. Like always. The world continued around her and she couldn't do a thing to participate, and in this case help get her family and friends out of trouble.

A slow burn rose up her chest. *Just stay out of trouble.* Is that what everyone thought? That Cassie had somehow caused this? She'd blamed herself from the beginning, yet Nate had almost convinced her she was not responsible for anything that had happened.

Bree was missing. Cassie's fault.

She narrowed her eyes at Agent Nance. "You were saying something before about helping me stop this madness?"

"You can start by calling Becca. We'll set up a meeting place."

"Are you going to arrest her?"

"Not if she cooperates."

"I should tell Chief Walsh."

"Let's get Becca into custody first. I'll convince her to give up Tony and testify against him. When the chief returns with evidence from the laundry facility, we'll have everything we need to shut this down. It will be over."

Finally. Cassie would be out of danger, her family, her friends...

Nate would be out of danger.

Cassie pulled out her phone and made the call.

Becca answered in a frantic state. "Cassie, I'm scared and now Tony's gone and I don't know where he is, and he said if he didn't come back to leave town but the bad guys will follow me!"

"Becca, listen, the FBI can protect you."

"They'll arrest me!"

"Agent Nance won't arrest you if you cooperate. I'm with him right now. Meet us somewhere so he can keep you safe."

"Tony said—"

"Stop listening to him. Hasn't he gotten you into enough trouble?"

The agent scribbled something on a piece of paper and slid it across the dining table.

"Bec, I'm sorry, I didn't mean to sound cross, but I'm worried about you, and my family."

"Your family?"

"Bree is missing. Becca, please help me. Meet me at—" she glanced at the slip of paper "—Sammish Park on Route Two, north end parking lot. Okay? Do you have a car?"

"I have your car."

"Can you meet us at the park in about—" She glanced at the agent.

"An hour," he said.

"In about an hour?" Cassie said to Becca.

"I don't know, maybe—"

"Becca, please, so no one else gets hurt. We can fix this, Bec. You and me."

"Okay."

Cassie pressed End and nodded at the agent. "She'll be there."

Nate contacted the local authorities to keep them in the loop about his investigation of Viceroy Laundry.

He pulled up to a large white building tucked away in the corner of an industrial park and double-checked the address.

A patrol car eased up next to him and an officer got out. "I'm Officer Panko with Mount Vernon PD."

"Chief Walsh, Echo Mountain."

They shook hands.

"My chief asked me to meet you here in case you needed assistance."

"Thanks." Nate eyed the building. "I'm a little surprised there's no signage identifying the company."

"Maybe because it's not a direct-to-consumer business?" the officer suggested.

"Perhaps." Nate and the young officer headed for the building.

"Can you tell me what this is about, Chief?"

"Smuggling bail jumpers out of the country. It's a federal case, but somehow landed in my town—" he glanced at Officer Panko "—and now yours."

"How did it lead you here?"

"They hide passports and cash in clean linen and deliver it to cabins. The criminals check in and it's waiting for them. What do you know about this place?"

They reached the front door.

"I've cruised by a few times," the officer said. "It never seemed occupied."

Hands cupped against the glass, Nate peered through the window into a reception area. The lights were off and no one was stationed behind the desk.

"Could you take that side of the building and I'll go around the other side?" Nate said.

"Sure, what am I looking for?"

"Signs of life, access inside. Finding an employee would be helpful."

"You got it."

Nate went around the left side of the building, peering through windows, trying to figure out if this was a legitimate company. It had to be since the linen was being washed and pressed somewhere before being stuffed with contraband, and delivered to Echo Mountain Rentals.

A crash echoed from the back of the building. Nate withdrew his gun. Could be nothing, but he wasn't taking any chances. He took a few more steps, ready to peer around the corner.

"Come on, faster!" a man shouted.

"Don't rush me," another answered. "Gotta set the timer."

"Just let 'er rip."

"Not until we're clear."

Wait a second, that sounded a lot like…they were setting a bomb?

"Police, freeze!" Officer Panko shouted.

Three shots rang out. Nate rushed around the corner and aimed his weapon.

Two men took cover behind a black SUV and opened fire. Nate darted back behind the building.

"Get in, get in!" one of the men shouted.

Nate peered into the parking lot and a bullet shattered the window above his head. He dodged back for cover, but not before he spotted Officer Panko on the ground.

Nate called for help. "Code Three. 8713 Industrial Boulevard. Send an ambulance, over."

Tires squealing, the SUV peeled out of the lot.

Nate aimed his weapon and hesitated in shock when he saw who was behind the wheel: Len Pragner.

How was that possible?

Nate refocused and fired, hitting the back quarter panel. The vehicle sped out of the parking lot. He got the make and model number and would call it in to Chief Washburn.

Just let 'er rip.

Not until we're clear.

Suspecting they'd set an incendiary device, Nate raced to Officer Panko. They had to get clear.

Nate didn't know how much time he had.

How big of an explosion to expect.

He grabbed Panko under the arms and dragged him across the parking lot behind a metal Dumpster. He did a quick check of the man's torso. No blood.

"Wore your vest. Smart kid," Nate said. Then he spotted blood staining his sleeve. He put pressure on the wound.

The wail of sirens filled the air. No, no, no, Nate had

to keep emergency vehicles away from the building, away from the—

An explosion rocked the ground. Nate automatically ducked as flying debris sailed over the Dumpster into the adjoining parking lot.

Officer Panko moaned and started to cough.

"It's okay," Nate said. "You're okay."

"What was that?"

"They destroyed the building." And with it, any leads to connect the mob to the smuggling operation.

Nate hung around for a few hours, hoping to get inside the demolished building, but local fire officials weren't giving anyone access because they deemed it unsafe.

"I doubt there's anything left between the incendiary devices and water damage," the fire chief said.

Nate offered him his business card. "Let me know if you find anything."

Nate headed back to Echo Mountain. His phone rang and he hoped it was Cassie calling to check in. He pressed the speakerphone button.

"Chief Walsh."

"Len Pragner has escaped," Detective Vaughn said. "They were transferring him from the hospital and two guys—"

"I know. He just blew up the laundry facility."

"You're kidding."

"Wish I were. How are you feeling?"

"I'm fine."

"She's not fine," Will said from the background. "She's taking the rest of the day off to bake cookies with me and the girls."

"Will, stop," she said.

Nate's phone beeped with another call. He glanced at the caller ID. "Chief Washburn's calling. Gotta take this."

"I'll check in later," she said.

"Sounds good." He switched over. "Chief?"

"You're not going to believe who owns a black SUV like the one that fled the scene of the explosion: Bill Anderson of Echo Mountain Rentals."

"We need to pick him up. Also, it was Len Pragner—"

"So you heard he's escaped."

"Yes. Send a patrol car to Anderson's home and I'll swing by his office."

"No, I'll go to his office—you need to get to the resort. Both McBride girls are missing."

SEVENTEEN

Cassie and the FBI agent anxiously waited for Becca. Three hours later, she was still a no-show. As twilight illuminated the mountain range in the distance, Cassie considered the fact that her friend had changed her mind, or worse—the mob guys had found her before Becca could get to Cassie.

Agent Nance spent much of his time making calls, pacing and looking worried. He asked Cassie to remain in the car, hidden from view.

She sensed he didn't appreciate her nonstop chatter, which was worse than usual because she was nervous, worried about Becca and Bree. She kept texting Aiden, asking if they'd found Bree, and he responded to stop bugging him.

She almost texted Nate, but didn't want to distract him. Even now, by helping the FBI track down Becca, a solid lead, Cassie didn't feel like she was doing nearly enough.

Agent Nance opened her car door. "Can I see your phone?"

"Sure, why?"

"We're going to try to trace Becca's phone."

"Oh, okay." She handed it to him and he walked a few feet away, holding his phone to his ear while analyzing the screen of hers.

Cassie, in the meantime, kept watch out the window, praying Becca was okay and that she would show up with a perfectly logical explanation as to why she took so long to get here. Optimism and prayer were Cassie's best defense against the panic threatening to drive her bonkers.

"Did they track her down?" she asked the agent.

"Not yet." He turned and glanced over the top of the car. "Someone's coming."

Cassie looked through the window. "It's Becca, driving my car." She started to get out.

"Wait," Nance said, putting out his hand.

Becca pulled up next to them. Cassie offered a wave, and got out of the agent's car. Becca opened the car door.

"I was so worried about you," Cassie said.

"I didn't know if I should come."

"I'm glad you did."

Agent Nance pulled Becca out of the car.

"Hey!" Cassie protested.

"Becca Edwards, you're under arrest." He cuffed her wrists in front.

"You said you weren't going to arrest her!" Cassie protested.

"We have to follow procedure, then offer her a deal." He read her her rights and led Becca to the back of Cassie's car.

"I didn't mean it, I didn't mean it." Becca sobbed.

Cassie was not liking this one bit.

"Let's see what you've got." Nance opened the trunk of Cassie's car. It was empty. He squeezed Becca's arm. "What did you do with it?"

"I didn't do anything. Let go, you're hurting me!"

"You and your boyfriend are done."

"Knock it off!" Cassie shouted, grabbing his arm.

Agent Nance was losing it, big-time, and he still had her phone so she couldn't call for help.

"Stop it!" Cassie said.

He shoved her away, just as...

A black SUV screeched into the parking lot. Three men got out, including Len Pragner. Cassie's heart dropped. The other two men aimed guns at Cassie, Becca and the FBI agent. A smile curled Len's lips.

"I'll take it from here, Agent Nance."

Nate tried not to break every speed law in the county as he raced back to the resort.

Cassie was missing.

When he tracked down Officer McBride, the cop was pacing the hallway outside Quinn's fortress apartment like a caged animal.

"What happened?" Nate said.

"I was helping search for Bree. Cassie told me to go, she told me she'd be fine with Agent Nance." Ryan hesitated. "He's FBI. He's good at protecting people, right?"

"Continue."

"I was gone maybe an hour. We found Bree in the shed outside. Someone locked her in and she was pounding and yelling, but it's way out there and—"

"And when you returned Cassie was gone?" Nate said, calmly.

"Both she and the agent were gone."

Nate whipped out his phone and called Agent Nance. It went directly to voice mail. He tried Cassie's phone. Again, voice mail. Needing to locate the agent, he called Chief Washburn. "Is Agent Nance at the police station?" Nate said.

"No, why?"

"He's missing, along with Cassie. We need to find them." Nate's forced calm was slowly slipping away.

"Maybe Bill Anderson will have answers. I just pulled up."

"On my way. Wait for me."

Nate glared at Officer McBride. "We need to find your cousin before they do. There's a guy at the resort, I think his name is Kyle. He's a tech genius. Check with Aiden. See if he can track her phone." Nate raced to his car.

At least they didn't toss Cassie and Becca out of a moving vehicle. What a morbid idea. But strange thoughts popped into your head when you faced death.

Regret whipped through Cassie as she considered what she'd be missing.

With Nate.

The man she should be spending the rest of her life with, a long life filled with laughter and children.

Children? She had never considered being a mother until she fell in love with Nate. A tear formed in her eye, but she swiped it away with her sleeve. She would be brave. She would not concede defeat just yet.

Len had put Cassie and Becca in the middle seat of the SUV as one of his men drove, and the other sat behind her and Bec. Cassie still couldn't quite believe they'd been taken hostage considering the way Len's men beat up the FBI agent, bound his wrists, and locked him in the trunk of Cassie's car.

Her empty car. Who could have stolen the linen from the trunk that hid contraband these violent men were after? A better question, what did Len and his mob friend want from Cassie and Becca?

"For the record," Len started, "I didn't kill that woman in the cabin."

Cassie thought his confession odd.

Len glanced at Cassie. "Not that I haven't killed before, but that was an accident."

"How was it an accident?" Cassie decided to placate him, try and make a connection.

"My boss sent me to the cabin to find her." He pointed at Becca. "She and her boyfriend have been stealing from us, and apparently kept stealing even when they knew we were after them."

"No, I didn't take the stuff in the trunk," Becca whimpered.

"Be that as it may, you'd better hope true love Tony returns it to us."

Becca shot a worried look at Cassie.

"What happened to Marilyn, the lady in the cabin?" Cassie redirected.

"I thought she was the property manager," Len said. "Didn't know what Becca looked like. Let myself in. The woman screamed and ran into the bathroom. Slipped and hit her head. Her mutt wouldn't shut up so I threw him in the closet."

"And the shovel?" Cassie said.

"Figured I'd dispose of the body. A murder would draw too much attention, and we weren't done with our business in town."

"Are you going to kill us?" she asked. Not knowing was the worst part.

Len frowned. "I have no reason to kill you, Cassie McBride."

"You chased me down—"

"I thought you were working with Becca and her brainless boyfriend."

"You were going to hurt me in the hospital, and at the farm and—"

"I wanted to find out where you stashed the money and passports. But you're not a part of this idiot scheme. You are not my enemy."

His bizarre integrity puzzled her considering who he worked for. Then again, maybe he was toying with her.

"I'm not naive," she said. "I've seen your faces."

Len burst out laughing, as if she'd told a joke.

"You watch too much television. It doesn't matter. Everyone knows who we are now, which is why guys like us need the passports, to start new lives somewhere." He patted his jacket pocket. "I always keep mine handy in case of emergency. But my friends here were supposed to get their new passports." He glared at Becca. "So we'll need those back."

He redirected his attention out the front window. Cassie studied her friend. Becca shook her head that she had no idea what happened to the laundry containing the contraband.

Cassie decided to be strong instead of scared.

"Len?"

He turned to her.

"How can I help?"

* * *

Nate got confirmation from the organized crime unit in Chicago that Wallingford Imports was tied to organized crime, and there had been communication with Echo Mountain Rentals.

Nate had his connection, a direct link from the mob to Bill Anderson. As they questioned Anderson, he pretended to be baffled by their accusations.

"I don't understand," he kept repeating.

"Drop the act," Nate said, fisting his hand. "You've been letting the mob use your cabins to smuggle bail jumpers out of the country."

Bill shook his head. "No, honestly. I don't know what you're talking about. Do I need a lawyer?"

"What you need is to help us find Cassie McBride before we add murder to your list of felonies," Nate said.

The front door opened and Carol entered the living room, holding a stack of files. "Oh, I'm sorry. I didn't know you had company, Bill."

"Come in," Nate said. "Maybe you can convince your boss to be straight with us."

"About what?" She laid her purse and files down on a table by the front door.

"They think I'm involved with the mob," Bill said in a panicked voice.

Carol's jaw dropped and her eyes widened.

"Carol, you know me better than anyone. Tell them they're wrong," Bill said.

Nate took a step toward Bill, towering over him as he shrank into the sofa. "People might die, today, because of you."

"Come on, Bill. We all make mistakes," Chief Washburn said, taking the soft approach.

Bill shook his head, looking genuinely dumbfounded.

This was going nowhere, and time was running out.

There had to be a way to break this guy. If only Nate could directly connect him to the evidence...

Of course, Detective Vaughn's stolen phone.

Bill must have taken it to prevent the police from acquiring evidence against him and the mob. Eyes focused on Bill, Nate took out his phone and hit Detective Vaughn's number.

A moment later, Vaughn's unique ring filled the room.

But it wasn't coming from Bill's pocket.

Nate slowly crossed the room, following the source of the sound. It originated from Carol's purse.

"Ma'am? The phone, please," Nate said.

She dug it out of her purse and handed it to him.

"I don't understand," Bill said.

"How did you get involved in this?" Nate asked.

The woman collapsed in an easy chair and burst into tears. Nate didn't have time for tears. He had to find Cassie.

"I'm sorry, I'm sorry," she said.

"Explain what's going on, please," Nate pressed. "And quickly."

"It's my grandson. He's in jail back in Chicago, and they said they'd protect him if I made sure the laundry was delivered and the reservations coincided with the deliveries." She looked at Nate. "Todd's the only family I have. I tried to get him to move out here with me, but he got caught up with a bad group of boys. He was so lost when his parents died."

"What was he incarcerated for?"

"Drug possession with intent to sell. He's not a tough kid, Chief. He was beaten up in jail and I thought they'd kill him. I had no choice."

Nate glanced at Chief Washburn and then knelt beside Carol. Threatening her with jail time wouldn't inspire her cooperation.

"Carol, I could call my contacts in Chicago to see what I can do to help your grandson, but you have to know that your days working with the mob in exchange for their protection are over."

She nodded.

"I'll make some calls, too, Carol," Chief Washburn offered. "But you need to help us."

"Please," Nate said, "I can't lose Cassie. Do you have any idea where Len would take her?"

She shook her head that she didn't. "I have Len's phone number and the laundry everyone's been looking for."

"Isn't it in Cassie's car?" Nate asked.

"No, I took it before it was towed from the rental office."

"And they think she still has it," Nate muttered.

A call came in and he answered, "I'm in the middle of—"

"They found Cassie McBride's car," Red said. "Agent Nance was stuffed into the trunk. Cassie and Becca were taken."

Two hours later Carol was scheduled to drop off the laundry with Len Pragner near an abandoned barn north of town. There was no reason Len would suspect she was working with the police.

Nate was careful whom he involved at this point. He no longer trusted Agent Nance, who admitted to persuading Cassie to help him bring in Becca even though it could be dangerous. Apparently Nance was tired of chasing his tail like the rest of them, and had planned to set a trap for Tony.

Using Becca and Cassie as bait.

Nate spoke with Agent Nance's boss, who wanted Nate to wait for federal agents before making the laundry drop. With Cassie's life in danger, Nate wasn't waiting on anyone. He said if the Feds wanted to close the mob smuggling case, they were welcome to pick up the perpetrators tomorrow morning at the Echo Mountain jail.

Nate, Chief Washburn, and Officers McBride and Carrington assembled at the meeting spot to go over the plan.

"I'll be in the backseat of Carol's car for protection," Nate said. "After she drops off the laundry, I'll get out of the car here—" Nate pointed to the map "—and hide in the trees.

I'll let you know when I see them approach. Radio County, they'll be waiting, and the three of you close ranks. These guys aren't going to be happy if they check the bag on site and find only laundry. If they do, we'll have minutes before they hurt Cassie and Becca."

Hurt them. He couldn't even think *kill them*.

"How many do you think will be in the SUV?" Mc-Bride said.

"I'm guessing two or three," Nate answered. "Everyone's wearing a vest?"

They all nodded.

"Let's focus on getting the hostages back unharmed."

Carol stood beside the car with a blank expression on her face.

"Carol?" Nate said.

She glanced at him. "Your help tonight will go a long way during your sentencing."

She nodded. "Love makes you do such stupid things."

Nate only hoped love *would not* make him stupid tonight.

Love. He loved Cassie.

"Nate?" Chief Washburn said.

Nate snapped his attention to the three men who looked to him for leadership and strength, men he knew attended Echo Mountain Church.

"I'd like to say a prayer," Nate uttered, surprising himself.

As they stood there, in the cool, quiet night, Nate led a short prayer asking for courage, strength and protection.

"Amen," they said, and took their positions.

The car rolled slowly across the uneven dirt road.

"You're doing great, Carol," Nate said, hiding in the backseat.

"I'm scared."

"It's okay, I'm here."

A few minutes later she stopped the car, got out and grabbed the laundry bag from the front seat.

"Quickly," Nate said.

She disappeared from view.

I'm coming, Cassie.

Carol returned, got behind the wheel and peeled out.

"Slow down. I need to jump out by the trees, remember?" Nate said.

"Right, sorry."

"Did you see anyone?"

"No."

"Chief Walsh, I see a black SUV parked on the south end of the barn, over," Red said through the radio.

"Ten-four."

Carol made a turn, out of view of the barn. Nate opened the door and jumped out, rolled, and took cover. He had a clear sight line of the white laundry bag.

As he hid in the trees, he felt like time passed so slowly, as if he'd been crouched there for hours, not minutes.

Out of the darkness, an SUV crawled toward the laundry. Closer, closer.

It stopped a good twenty feet from the bag.

A door opened.

Cassie, hands bound in front, got out of the SUV.

"I have a visual, over," Nate said in the calmest voice he could manage. "It's Cassie."

She walked slowly across the wide open space, as if she fully expected an assault.

Just as she reached the bag…

A car screeched across the property, heading directly toward her. Nate automatically stood.

He recognized the driver: Tony.

"Move in, everyone move in!" he ordered, and charged into the open field.

It was like everything clicked into slow motion. Cars were honking, people were shouting, and Cassie was fro-

zen in place, inches from the white laundry bag she was
sent to retrieve.

"Cassie, grab the bag and get in!" Becca called from the
open truck door.

All Cassie could do was stare at the bright lights blind-
ing her.

Gunshots pierced the night air, ripping her out of her
trance. Had Len changed his mind and decided to kill her?

She took off running, even though she doubted she could
outrun a car, or a bullet.

Someone tackled her and threw her to the ground. She
fought him at first, and then recognized the woodsy scent.

Nate.

The man she loved.

"You're okay," he said.

The sound of screeching tires was followed by a crash.

"Freeze, police!" someone shouted.

Multiple gunshots pierced the night air, then silence.
The sound of sirens, the wonderful sound of sirens echoed
across the field.

Relief edged its way into her heart, not only because
of the sirens, but because Nate held her close, physically
shielding her with his body, protecting her life with his own.

"Okay, I give up!" a man called. It wasn't Len Pragner,
it was one of his thugs.

New worry flooded her stomach. Had Len escaped the
SUV? Was he coming after her?

"We're clear, Chief!" her cousin Ryan called.

She peeked around Nate's arm and saw Len sprawled on
the ground, blood staining his shirt. One of his men lay a
few feet away, and the third man was in handcuffs, pinned
to the SUV by her cousin.

"Where's Becca? I'll kill him! I'll kill him!" Tony
shouted, racing toward Len's motionless body.

"Calm down," Officer Carrington ordered, shoving him
against the car and cuffing him.

"I'm here," Becca said, edging out of the SUV.

Cassie released a sigh. Her friend was okay and the mob guys were no longer a threat.

Chief Washburn rushed up to Cassie and Nate.

"Is she okay?" he asked.

"Cassie?" Nate said, with a concerned voice.

She turned and looked into his emerald-green eyes.

"Are you okay?" he said softly.

"Yes. As long as you don't let go."

EIGHTEEN

The next day at the police station, Cassie gave her official statement about what happened when Len had taken her hostage. She noticed Nate repeatedly clench and unclench his jaw as she told the story.

Mom, Bree and Aiden demanded to go along. Cassie had a feeling that after everything that had happened, her family was going to be even more protective than usual.

"What is with people? Are they stupid?" Aiden said, shaking his head. "What were Tony and Becca thinking?"

"We all make mistakes, not that you'd understand, Mr. Perfect," Cassie teased.

"Money is a powerful motivator," Nate said. "Tony thought money would solve all his problems and he'd get the girl."

Nate glanced up briefly at Cassie, and then he looked away.

Nate had his girl. He had to know that.

"I'm so glad it's over," her mom said. "It is over, right, Chief?" When she addressed her question to Chief Washburn, he pointed at Nate.

"He's the chief."

"Of course." She glanced down.

"Mom?" Cassie prodded. "Do you have something to say?"

She snapped her attention to Nate. "I'm sorry, you know how people talk. Once Chief Washburn came back, they thought, well..."

"That I couldn't handle my job?" Nate offered.

Her mom shrugged.

"Mo-ther," Cassie admonished.

"I didn't say it. I'm just repeating what I've heard."

"Well, I'd appreciate you repeating this," Chief Washburn started. "If it weren't for Nate, the town would still be in danger. He's the one who pieced it together. He figured out Carol was the mob's contact in Echo Mountain. And he's the one who threw himself into the line of fire to save Cassie's life."

"That's my job, to protect the citizens of Echo Mountain," Nate said.

Cassie didn't like the sound of that. She was more than an ordinary citizen, wasn't she?

Aiden extended his hand to Nate. "Thanks, buddy."

"Wait, so Carol was a part of this scheme because...?" her mom asked.

"The mob was providing protection for her grandson who was incarcerated." Nate turned to Cassie. "I'm surprised Len was so forthcoming with you about the supposed accidental death of Marilyn Brandenburg, and giving you details of how their operation worked."

"It was strange, but on some level I think he had his own measure of integrity."

Aiden snorted. "Come on, Cassie, you can't be *that* naive after all this."

"Everything isn't just black or white, Aiden. There are shades of gray, ya know," she countered.

"The FBI agent was definitely gray," Bree said. "I can't believe he bamboozled me into thinking Cassie was in the shed, then locked me in."

"I also suspect he spiked my coffee at Healthy Eats," Nate said. "Which is why I nearly passed out while driving. He'd hoped I would question my ability to keep Cassie safe and turn her over to him. He wanted to be in charge from day one."

"He manipulated me into helping him draw out Becca," Cassie said. She looked at Nate. "I am sorry about that."

"What are you sorry about?"

"That I went with him when you told me to stay at the resort. I was so desperate to put an end to all this violence."

"Well, it's over now. The Feds will take Tony, Becca, Carol and the mob guys into custody."

"Poor Becca," Cassie said.

"And Carol," her mom added.

"Why did she have the linens?" Cassie said.

"Carol was considering her options, turning the evidence over to the Feds in exchange for her grandson's safety, or continuing to work with the mob. She was playing a dangerous game," Nate explained.

"Because of her poor grandson," Mom offered. "How long do you think she'll be in jail?"

"If she and Becca cooperate, their sentences could be reduced, but Tony, he'll be going away for a while," Nate said.

"I know Becca is desperate to make amends," Cassie said.

Aiden's phone beeped and he glanced at it. "Gotta go."

"We should let the chief get back to work," Mom said, touching Cassie's arm. "Ready?"

"I've got some things to do in town."

"If you think we're letting you out of our sight, you're wrong," her mom said.

"Mom—"

"She's right, Cassie. You must be traumatized," Bree said. "Move back in with Mom for a while. I'll come by for dinner and—"

Cassie stood. "No."

Her mom's eyes widened, Bree's jaw dropped, and Aiden froze at the door, turned and looked at Cassie.

Nate shot Cassie an encouraging nod.

"I love you guys," Cassie started. "I love you so much, but you tend to smother me, probably because of my illness, and now because of the last few days. I get it, I do. I appreciate how much you love me, so much so that you always want to help."

"Cassie—"

"Please, let me say this," she interrupted her mom. "I successfully escaped a killer, talked rationally to him and stayed alive until help arrived." She smiled at Nate. "I'm a mature woman, and would like to be treated like one. I don't know any other way to put it but—" she hesitated and made eye contact with Mom, Aiden and Bree "—the way you love me can be stifling."

"That's unfair," Aiden said.

"Aiden," Mom said. "Let her finish."

Cassie took her mom's hand. "You're the greatest mom a girl could have. Have faith in your parenting skills, and give me some space. Sure, I'll stumble and fall, but that's the best way to learn, right?"

Tears formed in her mom's eyes, and Cassie momentarily regretted speaking her truth.

Mom reached out and hugged her. "I couldn't be more proud."

Cassie hugged her back, a little surprised. Bree squeezed her shoulder and offered a smile.

"Okay, whatever," Aiden said. "I have no idea what's going on. Does anyone need a ride?"

All three women said, "No." Then burst into giggles.

"Women," Aiden muttered, shaking his head.

"Just give us a minute, Aiden." Mom broke the hug and studied Cassie. "I had no idea you felt this way."

Cassie smiled. "Yeah, well, a friend taught me to speak my truth."

"I'm so glad she did."

"He," Cassie corrected.

"Oh, do tell," Mom said.

"Come on, Mom, let's go," Bree encouraged.

"I'll walk you ladies out," Chief Washburn said.

"I'll text you later," Cassie said.

"Call me later," Mom countered.

"I'll teach you how to text, Mom," Bree said.

"What if I don't want to text? I like to hear the sound of my children's voices."

"Then Cassie can send you a voice message," Bree said as Chief Washburn held the door open for them.

"You mean her real voice or a robot voice? I don't like those robot voices, like that phone lady. She sounds so stern," Mom said before the door closed on them.

Cassie glanced at Nate, and he smiled.

"Well done," he said.

"Thanks. Is there anything else you need from me?"

His smile faded. Tension filled the room.

"No, I think we're good." He stood as if he intended to walk her to the door.

But Cassie was not done talking, nor was she done showing him how she felt. Confessing to her family gave her strength and a new sense of confidence.

She stepped up to Nate, hugged him and pressed her cheek against his chest. "Thank you."

"It's my job."

"Teaching me to find my voice? That's not in the police chief's job description."

"It's in my 'friend' job description."

"Come on, we both know there's more to this than friendship."

She felt pressure against her shoulders. He was pushing her away. She leaned back and looked into his troubled green eyes, but she didn't let go. "What's wrong?"

"It's over, Cassie. You're safe, free to take your trips and follow your dream."

She was not letting him push her away.

Speak your truth.

"Nate, I care about you, a lot."

"I know. I heard you in the cabin when you thought I was unconscious."

Heat rose to her cheeks. "You did?"

"Yes."

"Huh. I don't know if I should be embarrassed or relieved." She studied his face. "Or worried?"

He shook his head. "There's no need to be worried. You're safe, remember?"

"I wasn't talking about the mob."

Nate wouldn't look into her eyes. Then reality hit her dead-on: he didn't share the same feelings. He truly had only been doing his job both as police chief, and as Aiden's good friend.

Nate didn't love her.

Suddenly embarrassed, she released him and grabbed her shoulder bag. "Right, okay, sorry."

"I thought we agreed you never had to say sorry, especially to me."

She glanced across the room at him. "I was simply saying I'm sorry that I misinterpreted your behavior. I'm sorry I'm so naive, so immature that I misread your signals." She hesitated. "Signals I guess I imagined."

When he didn't correct her, she glanced through the window at the bakery across the street. A young couple walked out holding hands. Her throat started to close with emotion.

What would make her think a man like Nate Walsh would want to commit his life to a naive Pollyanna like Cassie? This thing between them was simply a young girl's romantic dream, a dream she'd never experienced in her teens because she didn't get out much due to her illness. She sighed and tried to focus on the good things that had come out of the past few days.

Nothing came to mind.

She'd originally thought the best thing had been the beauty of romantic love blossoming between her and Nate.

She'd fallen deeply in love for the first time and it felt amazing. Until now.

Why can't he love me?

The ball in her throat grew, threatening to cut off her voice. Cassie needed to escape his office.

She glanced at her phone. "Whoa, it's almost noon. I forgot I'm interviewing a pet sitter about watching Dasher while I'm gone." She zipped her coat. "I'm thinking two weeks in Europe will be a good test run to see where I'd like to spend more of my time. But you know Bree and Mom, they'll worry no matter where I go," she chatted away, not paying attention to what she was saying.

"Of course they'll worry. They love you," Nate said.

But you don't.

Her heart splintered into tiny pieces as she meandered to the door. Without looking at him again for fear she'd lose it, she started to say something trite in farewell, but stopped herself.

Her last words to the man she loved would not be pithy or disrespectful of her own feelings. She opened the door and said, "God bless."

She rushed outside and motored down Main Street. It didn't take long for the tears to break free.

Maybe this was a necessary lesson before she left on her trip. Perhaps she needed to experience heartbreak before she encountered men in a foreign land. Having her heart broken by Nate—the man she would have given up traveling for—would make her more discerning and guarded. A good thing, right?

She bumped into someone on the street. "Sorry," she said and continued walking.

"Cassie?"

She swiped at her eyes and turned around. Nate's sister, Catherine, studied her with a puzzled frown.

"Are you okay?" she asked.

"Sure, fine. Just late, sorry." Cassie practically sprinted away from her. Oh great, now the entire town of Echo Mountain would know she was blubbering her way down Main Street like a little girl, a child who'd lost her best friend, which in a sense she had.

Suddenly, she couldn't get out of town fast enough.

Nate leaned back in his office chair, staring at the door. It was the only way, the best way. If he'd been honest with

Cassie and admitted he loved her, she might shelve her dream of seeing the world and experiencing new things.

He would not be responsible for holding her back.

Besides, she was young at heart, not cynical like Nate. She deserved more than an emotionally damaged cop as a partner in life.

He considered everything she'd done for him, showing him light where he could see only darkness, and opening his heart to a loving, forgiving God, something he'd never even considered before he'd spent time with Cassie.

God, please take care of her.

He worried about her, the way she'd rushed out of his office wearing that strained smile, the one she'd used on her family when they hovered and she wanted them gone.

The office door burst open and his sister stomped her feet on the mat.

"Hey, shouldn't you be at work?" he said.

Catherine stormed across the room and dropped a brown paper bag onto his desk. "This *was* for you, but now I'm reconsidering."

"What is it?" He reached for the bag.

She slapped his hand. "Double chocolate mini muffins, your favorite." She glared at him with steely green-gray eyes. "What did you do to her?"

"Her, who her?"

"Cassie McBride."

"I didn't do anything, other than protect her from the mob."

"Don't be a smarty Sam. You're as bad as Dylan," she said. "Now, come on, it's obvious that girl is crazy about you, overlooking your rough edges and bossy nature. She even made you smile in public. I've seen it." She crossed her arms over her chest.

"Is there a question here?"

"What did you just say to her?"

"I didn't say anything."

She snatched the bag of mini muffins. "Then why was she so upset? She was bawling her eyes out."

He fisted his hand. He knew he'd hurt her, but hearing it from his sister made it all the more painful.

"I can't give her what she needs," he said softly.

"Is that what you said to her?"

"Not exactly, no."

"Of course not, because you know she'd talk you out of such nonsense. What do you think she needs, Nate, huh?"

"To get out of town and travel, live her dream. She's earned that right."

"She's also earned the right to fall in love and be loved in return. Are you seriously telling me you don't love that adorable woman?"

"I never said that."

"Then you *do* love her?"

"Can I have my muffins?"

"Answer the question."

"Yes, I love her. That's why I'm letting her go."

"You mean, you didn't tell her the truth, that you love her?"

"I didn't want to confuse her."

"She's a grown woman. Don't you think it's up to her to decide? No, of course not, because you're Nate the great, the police chief, the guy who's going to make everything right for everyone." She turned to leave.

"Catherine—"

"Stop." She whirled on him. "You've always challenged me to speak my truth, yet you can't tell Cassie how you feel because you're afraid she'll make the wrong decision. Wrong in whose eyes? Yours?"

"You don't understand."

"Sure I do. You don't think you're a good enough reason for her to stay in town. Well, guess what, that's her decision to make. Stop trying to control everything, and stop hurting the love of your life out of some warped sense of sacrifice." With a shake of her head, his sister marched toward the door. "If you love and respect her you'll be honest instead of treating her like a child."

"I'm not treating her like—"

"Swallow your pride and apologize for being a blockhead. 'I'm sorry.' It's two words. And she's earned them."

Catherine left and slammed the door.

He tipped back his office chair, considering Catherine's lecture. Had he been treating Cassie like a child, making decisions for her like her own family had over the past twenty-five years?

Or was this something more?

You don't think you're a good enough reason for her to stay in town.

Deep down he felt Cassie deserved better than what Nate could offer. Was that a good enough reason to keep the truth from her, the truth that he loved her with all his heart?

Here he'd been challenging her to speak her truth to her family, yet he'd refused to be truthful with Cassie. What a hypocrite. That certainly wasn't what an honorable man would do, or a man searching for grace.

He sighed. *Lord, I love her. Please show me the way.*

Her family and friends wanted to throw Cassie a party at Healthy Eats Restaurant, a combination "celebrate life" and "bon voyage" party.

She wasn't in a celebratory mood. It had been only a few days since they'd closed the smuggling case, a few tense days of keeping herself busy and trying to ignite enthusiasm about her future travels.

For the first time in her life, her heart wasn't in it.

"I guess that's what heartbreak does to ya," she said to Dasher, who snoozed in a doggy bed in the corner of her apartment.

Sure, she'd shopped flights to London, but she hadn't done much else, nor had she officially booked anything.

The party was meant to be a celebration of life, of making it through dangerous waters and coming out safely on shore.

Which she couldn't have done without Nate's help.

A part of her wanted to get a cab, catch a flight out of Sea-Tac and disappear. No, that was childish. But she wasn't sure what to expect at the party tonight and didn't want to show up in a sour mood when the guests were cheering her on and wishing her safe travels.

"I'd better not be late for my own party," she said to Dasher. The dog didn't stir, his little paws twitching as if he was having a very good dream, probably about racing through an open field.

Cassie slipped into nice black pants and a colorful top. She grabbed her purple shoulder bag and headed to the restaurant.

There were only three cars in the parking lot, and the blinds were closed. Did she get the date wrong? Was she late? Catherine had said eight o'clock.

She got out of her car and approached the restaurant. A sign was taped to the door: "Come in and celebrate!"

Cassie stepped inside. The lights were low, and soft music drifted across the restaurant.

An empty restaurant.

"Catherine?" Cassie said.

Instead, Nate stepped out of the kitchen. Dressed in a suit jacket, white shirt and jeans, he gripped a bouquet of flowers.

Cassie's breath caught in her throat.

"It's just you and me tonight," he said. "I hope that's okay."

"Sure, okay."

He closed the distance between them and offered her the flowers.

"They're beautiful," she said, loving the bright purples and pinks.

He motioned to a table covered in a white linen cloth, with delicate china plates and tulip-shaped water glasses.

Nate pulled out a chair and she sat down, still clinging to the flowers.

He joined her at the table and smiled. "Like the music?"

She nodded that she did, still trying to make sense of what was happening.

"Oh, and I got you something else." He opened a small white box and slid it across the table. "A charm to add to your key chain."

"It's the Swiss flag," she said, breathless. He remembered she wanted a charm to represent Switzerland.

"How about a drink?" he offered.

She nodded, unable to speak coherently.

"Hey, sis?" he called.

Catherine came into the dining room carrying a pitcher. "Fresh apple-carrot-kale juice with a hint of ginger." She filled their glasses.

"Cassie, can I put the flowers in water for you?" she offered.

Cassie handed her the bouquet, still speechless. Catherine disappeared into the kitchen.

"I'll bet you're wondering what all this is about," Nate said, studying her.

Cassie nodded that she was, in fact, wondering.

He smiled. "Wow, you're actually speechless."

"I don't want to ruin it," she blurted out.

"No." He sighed. "But I almost did." He pinned her with loving green eyes. "I'm sorry."

"For…?"

"For not being truthful, for trying to protect you and ending up making decisions for you."

"I'm confused."

"I love you."

Her jaw dropped.

"You had to see that coming," Nate said.

"Yes, but no…but yes?"

He reached across the table for her hand. She offered it, never wanting to let go.

"I love you so much I didn't want to ruin your dream of traveling, of going on your adventures."

"Being with you is an adventure."

"I'm not sure if that's a compliment or—"

"It is. You've made me forget my need to escape. You've taught me to speak my truth. I thought that's what love looked like."

"You were right. And I was a jerk, a bossy jerk, according to my sister."

"You've never been bossy with me," Cassie said. "You've been kind and encouraging and supportive. We are good together."

"What about your travels?"

"Traveling would be more fun if I had an adventurous travel buddy."

"I might know just the guy."

"Oh, really?" She smiled.

"If you can wait a year. I'll have earned more vacation time by then."

Cassie got up and went to Nate. "My love," she said, "take all the time you need. I'm not going anywhere."

She leaned in for a gentle kiss.

And in that moment, all her dreams had come true.

* * * * *

Dear Reader,

I'm so very excited to present to you the fifth book in my Echo Mountain series, featuring Cassie McBride and Police Chief Nate Walsh. What a great couple!

Cassie is an optimist with a lighthearted nature who's paired with Nate, the strong silent type who intimidates people just by looking at them. Yet somehow, as Nate plays bodyguard for Cassie in the rugged Cascade Mountains, they help each other work through their personal struggles, and Cassie opens Nate's heart to the concept of "grace."

The emotionally guarded chief of police even challenges Cassie to speak her truth with love to her family, something she's been unable to do. She'd rather escape her hometown and travel indefinitely than tell her mom, brother and sister that their smothering style is driving her away. But before she can speak her truth, Cassie must elude mob guys who think she has taken something of theirs. As Cassie and Nate spend time together, he feels saddened by the thought of losing her once the case is solved and she leaves town. But if he loves her, he won't hold her back from her dream of traveling.

The theme of speaking your truth with love is woven throughout the pages of this book because I feel it's essential for healthy relationships. I hope you enjoyed Cassie and Nate's journey as they learned to come together and embrace truth and faith.

Peace,
Hope White

COMING NEXT MONTH FROM
Love Inspired® Suspense

Available October 4, 2016

IDENTITY UNKNOWN
Northern Border Patrol • by Terri Reed
When Nathanial Longhorn washes up on deputy sheriff Audrey Martin's beach—followed by men intent on killing him—he has no memory. And Audrey is the only one he trusts to protect him as he recovers his past.

HIGH-RISK REUNION
Lone Star Justice • by Margaret Daley
Someone is out for revenge against district attorney Tory Carson. And they're willing to hurt her teenage daughter to get to her. But Tory's former love, Texas Ranger Cade Morgan, will do whatever it takes to keep them both safe.

LAKESIDE PERIL
Men of Millbrook Lake • by Lenora Worth
Chloe Conrad suspects foul play in the plane crash that killed her sister—and she hires private investigator Hunter Lawson to prove it. But when their investigation puts both of their lives in jeopardy, can they find the truth before they become the next victims?

TARGETED FOR MURDER
Wilderness, Inc. • by Elizabeth Goddard
Chased by assassins after her secret agent father's death, Hadley Mason flees into the Oregon wilderness to disappear. But when killers catch up with her, Hadley's life rests in the hands of Cooper Wilde, a wilderness-survival teacher who's determined to defend her.

KIDNAPPED AT CHRISTMAS • by Maggie K. Black
When journalist Samantha Colt is kidnapped and wakes up on her boss's porch, she can't remember how she got there. Somebody wants to harm her, and her boss's house sitter, soldier Joshua Rhodes, puts his life on the line to guard her.

DEADLY SETUP • by Annslee Urban
Set on clearing her brother's name, Paige Becker returns home...and finds herself a killer's next target. Now she must rely on her ex-boyfriend Seth Garrison—the detective who arrested and charged her brother with murder—to save her life.

LOOK FOR THESE AND OTHER LOVE INSPIRED BOOKS WHEREVER BOOKS ARE SOLD, INCLUDING MOST BOOKSTORES, SUPERMARKETS, DISCOUNT STORES AND DRUGSTORES.

LISCNM0916

REQUEST YOUR FREE BOOKS!

2 FREE RIVETING INSPIRATIONAL NOVELS
PLUS 2 FREE MYSTERY GIFTS

Love Inspired®
SUSPENSE
RIVETING INSPIRATIONAL ROMANCE

YES! Please send me 2 FREE Love Inspired® Suspense novels and my 2 FREE mystery gifts (gifts are worth about $10). After receiving them, if I don't wish to receive any more books, I can return the shipping statement marked "cancel." If I don't cancel, I will receive 4 brand-new novels every month and be billed just $4.99 per book in the U.S. or $5.49 per book in Canada. That's a savings of at least 17% off the cover price. It's quite a bargain! Shipping and handling is just 50¢ per book in the U.S. and 75¢ per book in Canada.* I understand that accepting the 2 free books and gifts places me under no obligation to buy anything. I can always return a shipment and cancel at any time. Even if I never buy another book, the two free books and gifts are mine to keep forever.

123/323 IDN GH5Z

Name	(PLEASE PRINT)	
Address		Apt. #
City	State/Prov.	Zip/Postal Code

Signature (if under 18, a parent or guardian must sign)

Mail to the **Reader Service**:
IN U.S.A.: P.O. Box 1867, Buffalo, NY 14240-1867
IN CANADA: P.O. Box 609, Fort Erie, Ontario L2A 5X3

Are you a current subscriber to Love Inspired® Suspense books and want to receive the larger-print edition?
Call 1-800-873-8635 or visit www.ReaderService.com.

* Terms and prices subject to change without notice. Prices do not include applicable taxes. Sales tax applicable in N.Y. Canadian residents will be charged applicable taxes. Offer not valid in Quebec. This offer is limited to one order per household. Not valid for current subscribers to Love Inspired Suspense books. All orders subject to credit approval. Credit or debit balances in a customer's account(s) may be offset by any other outstanding balance owed by or to the customer. Please allow 4 to 6 weeks for delivery. Offer available while quantities last.

Your Privacy—The Reader Service is committed to protecting your privacy. Our Privacy Policy is available online at www.ReaderService.com or upon request from the Reader Service.
We make a portion of our mailing list available to reputable third parties that offer products we believe may interest you. If you prefer that we not exchange your name with third parties, or if you wish to clarify or modify your communication preferences, please visit us at www.ReaderService.com/consumerschoice or write to us at Reader Service Preference Service, P.O. Box 9062, Buffalo, NY 14240-9062. Include your complete name and address.

LIS15